P9-CAB-495

For Mike

For Mike

—Shelley Sykes—

Delacorte Press

Published by
Delacorte Press
Bantam Doubleday Dell Publishing Group, Inc.
1540 Broadway
New York, New York 10036

Library of Congress Cataloging-in-Publication Data

Sykes, Shelley.
For Mike / Shelley Sykes.
p. cm.
Summary: When Jeff's best friend Mike disappears in the fall of their senior year in high school, Jeff has disturbing dreams in which Mike urges him to come get him, and a secret begins to unfold.
ISBN 0-385-32337-9
[1. Dreams—Fiction. 2. Ghosts—Fiction. 3. Mystery and detective stories.] I. Title.
PZ7.S9834Fo 1998
[Fic]—dc21
97-23452
CIP
AC

The text of this book is set in 12.5-point Goudy.

Book design by Ericka Meltzer
Manufactured in the United States of America

April 1998

10 9 8 7 6 5 4 3 2 1
BVG

This is for Evan Hunter.

Thanks go to Lieutenant Michael Weir, Station Commander, and the Pennsylvania State Police Troopers of Troop H, Gettysburg Station. They answered my questions with such patience.

I also need to thank my critique group, who can be hard; my editor, Wendy, who can be harder; and my family, who can be hardest of all.

Chapter 1

Somehow I knew it was a dream.

But knowing you're in a dream doesn't make it any less potent, does it? And this dream, well, this was welcome in a way, because I could hear Mike calling my name and I knew that if I kept going around corners I'd eventually run into him. Then I could ask him where the hell he'd been for almost three weeks.

"Jeff! You've gotta help me out, man," Mike called.

I had tunnel vision, and the halls were like the halls in school, only the school's halls didn't snake and turn like these. And the school's floors didn't tip to the right.

"Mike, where are you?"

"Jeff . . ."

I turned a corner and there he was. "What the hell happened to you, man?"

He laughed and ran a hand over his head. His face was split by shadow; the side I could see was streaked with mud and his tangled brown hair had bits of leaves and twigs in it. The clothes he wore, ripped-knee jeans and a flannel shirt unbuttoned over a black tee, were damp. I could only see one of his dark brown eyes, and bright light from beside us made that eye glisten like crystal.

"Yeah, well," he said. "Help me out?"

It was the way he would ask for a lift, or for help in algebra. *"Help me out?"*

"Sure, Mike. But where've you been?"

"Get Kirby. Then come get me."

"Where are you, Mike?"

"I'm nowhere, man," he said with a laugh that sent a cold feeling around my neck. "Nowhere yet. Come get me."

"Okay. We're looking for you. You know that, right?"

"Get Kirby and come get me."

"Okay, Mike," I said. Then I watched as he began slapping at his chest. Light, flat-palmed slaps. "What are you doing?"

"I lost it, man! Now I'm nowhere. 'S not fair, Jeff."

"Mike, don't." I moved to take his wrist, but he backed away. Not slow, but with a *whoosh,* and then I was sitting up, in the dark of my room. It was the second time in two days that I'd dreamed the same thing.

I looked at the green glow of my digital clock: 2:15 in the morning. Mike had been gone since the end of September. It would be three weeks on Thursday since I'd said, "See you," like I always did when I left school. I'd had no idea that I'd be one of the last people who could pinpoint his whereabouts that day. If I had known, maybe I would have paid more attention to the way he'd pulled a hand out of his pocket and held it up to wave. Was it my imagination, or had he seemed quieter? Sad? Afraid, even?

"Stop," I said aloud, and fell backward on the bed. Mike was my best friend. If something had been wrong, he would have told me. Then why? I asked myself, the argument old and memorized by now, if nothing was wrong, why did he disappear?

Something must have happened to him. Something bad.

No way. I can't let myself think that way.

Then think he ran away. It's easier to think he just upped and went away.

Yeah, that's good. He went away.

Why? He would have told you.

Yeah, he would have. Something must have happened to him. Something bad.

I groaned and rolled onto my stomach, pulling the blankets over my head. Mike and I were going to have the best senior year ever, hadn't we said so? I was planning for college, and Mike, considering all avenues, had even mentioned the navy. Now, here I was, dreaming about him at night and thinking about how he wanted me to get Kirby and come get him.

Kirby. Jerry Kirby was a guy we'd hung around with for

quite a while. He was loud; "on the edge" is how Mike described him. Talking about racing cars and drinking his dad's liquor when he had a chance. But he was okay and we got along. Still, I couldn't figure out why Mike was asking me to bring Kirby into my dreams. How could I tell somebody like Kirby that I was having dreams about Mike?

I don't know, Mike, I thought. I don't know if I can tell Kirby. And if I do, where are we supposed to go to get you? I heard Mike's voice again just like in the dream. "I'm nowhere, man. Nowhere."

I listened to it over and over in my head, and grew sleepy under the blanket.

I was still thinking about the dream the next day at lunch. As usual, the cafeteria was noisy and Amy was yapping to her friend. Not wanting to talk, I didn't try to stop her. I didn't want to hear every detail of her morning, which, come on, except for cheerleading practice, was exactly like mine.

I yawned midchew and watched Kirby across the cafeteria, struck as always by the paradox he presented. He was tall and muscular, always working out and obsessed with his body. Words like *gladiator* and *warrior* could very easily be used when describing him. But I could never understand how someone so obsessed with himself could treat the inside of his body as badly as Kirby did. He paid more attention to what was going on his whitish blond hair than to what he let into his stomach or lungs.

He was laughing with somebody and I remembered the night last winter when he, Mike, and I went sledding down Harmon's Hill on the hood of an '85 Chevy Cavalier.

Kirby's dad runs the Auto Recycling Center. In the good old days it was called a towing and wrecking service. We scrounged a fairly smooth hood from the fenced-off lot, tied a rope to it, and dragged it the half mile to the hill. It was a great sled, and the quarter-mile run was worth the long haul to the top.

But Kirby could always make something worthwhile, no matter what hassle it took. On the day after his eighteenth birthday, just before school started, Mike and I were helping him clean out a fire circle in the field behind the garage. We cut down weeds, dug it out, raked it, and then went to look for rocks to set around it. That's when Kirby decided he had to go get the food and drinks.

So Mike and I sweated in the sun, dragging rocks and wondering why Kirby was taking so long. It was finished by the time he came back, of course. But that night, while we roasted hot dogs with the others who showed up for the party, Kirby gave all the credit to us. He was an okay guy.

Mike had been getting odd parts from Kirby, cheap, to

fix up his dad's old Chevy. I had doubts that the car would be done anytime this decade, but Mike enjoyed working on it. It sat in a garage behind his house.

Now Kirby got up and tossed his milk carton into the recycling bin. He glanced my way, caught my eye, and waved. I almost called him over, but he turned and started through the doors before I could. He'd pretty much stayed away from me since word about Mike had gotten around. I figured he preferred Mike to me, or maybe he felt uncomfortable.

Lots of people acted uncomfortable around me now. I mean, they would come up and ask, "Have you heard anything?" Then, when I had to say, "No," they'd sort of shrug and slink away. It bugged me, in a way, this coming to me for answers. But I understood it. I was, after all, Mike's best friend, and his disappearance was like *the biggest deal* at school.

It had surprised me—all the people who came to ask—though it shouldn't have. Mike was a quiet guy who somehow got pulled into the hub from the edge of the wheel. People liked him, noticed him. In turn, Mike could find his place in any group: jocks, artists, or underdogs. I never knew who I'd find him deep in conversation with while he waited on the bleachers as I ran track: a cheerleader, the class president, or the fat kid from the sports video department.

Amy had told me last week, "You look so darn sad, Jeff."

Well, tough.

I looked at her. She's pretty, and she says her auburn hair is naturally wavy. She's a real nice girl. So I wondered when I had quit feeling anything special for her.

Mike had looked at me like I was naked, when I'd told him my problem. "What?" he'd said, peeling the earphones off his head even though I knew he'd heard me. He swung his legs off the side of his bed and stared at me openmouthed. "But you said she was perfect, Jeff. What's happened?"

"I don't know. It's just not like it was, that's all."

"Did you sleep together? Or something?" He shook his head, answering his own question.

"No. She's just so . . . different. We don't talk like we used to, or even make out like we used to. I hear about the new sweater and where we're going to go so she can wear it, and it's more like I'm a convenience."

"Convenience?"

"Like she would say, 'My car, my job, my favorite store, my boyfriend-slash-date.' "

"So? That's what you are. It's no different from saying you're my friend."

"Yes it is." I didn't try to tell Mike that when I looked into the future Amy was nowhere in sight. That it wasn't like with Mike, who'd always be there.

"Have you talked to her about it?"

"I tried a couple of times. Once she said, 'You look so serious, come on. We're going to be late.' "

Mike pouted for effect and slid the earphones over my head, turning the volume up.

That was about a week before Mike disappeared. Now the problem with Amy had been shelved and I really didn't feel like thinking about it. But I couldn't tell her about the dream.

Then I saw Berry Murphy.

Berry was a year behind me, a junior. I'd known her forever. Our dads were with the State Police, and she was as much a part of our family as I was of hers. Years ago we kind of developed a crush on each other, but it went away when I started high school. In the meantime, though, we'd found out we had a lot in common. For instance, we both had Cop's Kid Syndrome.

There was one interest we didn't share. Berry used to talk about things like ESP and ghosts and dreams all the time. I could still remember one summer night when we were watching for meteors and she talked about the universe and how she'd go exploring it in her afterlife. I'd thought it was nuts then, and I still have my doubts, but at least she would be a starting point.

I nudged Amy in the ribs. "I have to talk to someone."

"Sure," she said with the bright-eyed look that all cheerleaders seem to wear. "I'll see you in English."

Berry was sitting with one of her friends, whose name slipped my mind.

Berry nodded at me. Her long, dark hair, which was

full of tight curls, rode up and down on her shoulder blades.

"Hey," I said as I sat down. I looked at her friend. "Hi. Millie, right?"

"Molly," Berry said, turning big hazel eyes to me. "What's up?"

I shrugged. "I was just wondering if you still read all that spooky stuff."

"Spooky stuff!"

"You know what I mean, Berry. All those books about ESP, ghosts . . . dreams."

She gave me a narrowed look. "Dreams and ghosts? You?"

"Look, forget it, all right?" I started to get up.

She put a hand on my arm. "Wait, Jeff. I've got lots of books. If you want to borrow some, just come on over. You're usually such a skeptic; you surprised me, that's all."

I sat back down. "Okay."

"Is that all you wanted?"

"Yup."

I sat there a minute and pretended not to listen to the conversation I'd interrupted.

I thought I'd drive over to her house that evening and maybe tell her about the dream. I didn't think she'd laugh at me. Hey, Mike, I thought, sorry about Kirby, but will Berry do? She knows about this stuff.

So in English class I told Amy I wouldn't be coming by after dinner like she'd asked me to.

"Why's that?"

"I need to go by Berry's after dinner."

"What for?"

It irked me that she seemed to think she was owed a reason. "You and I don't have any firm plans anyway."

"Then come later, after you have your talk."

"Why can't we just skip tonight? I've got homework."

"I want to discuss our costumes for the party. I was—"

"Amy . . ."

Her dark eyes went wide and she closed her mouth.

I knew I'd committed one of the cardinal sins according to Amy. Interrupting her just wasn't done. She crossed her arms and sat back.

"I don't know if I'll be over later or not," I said. "I don't even know if I want to go to that party now. I'll have to call you."

"I don't know if I'll sit around and wait on your call, Jeff," she said, and began to copy things from the board.

There it was. The set jaw that signaled the old silent treatment. Geez, you'd think girls would change punishments around a little, just to keep you on your toes. But they pick a favorite and stick to it.

"Amy, I said I'll call when I make up my mind."

She huffed. "That's part of the problem, Jeff. I never know what to count on. You said we'd go to Chad's party and now you don't know. Well, I'm going, whether you go or not."

I sighed. I should have apologized and tried to explain, but I didn't have it in me.

In my mind I saw Mike's put-on pout.

Chapter 2

One time Dad talked about a man he helped arrest. The guy had a look in his eyes that Dad said was a mixture of relief and completion, as if the guy was saying, "This is it then, isn't it?"

As I drove to Berry's house I was thinking about the way Amy had looked at me when school let out. There had been something of that same look in her eyes, and I knew the thing about the party had been an ultimatum. I had spent fifteen minutes wondering why it didn't bother me, and had to give up.

Mike had never been serious about any one girl and had always nagged me about concentrating on a relationship instead of just having fun like him.

"I wouldn't be comfortable," he said once. I wasn't sure of his meaning, but I figured it pertained to the way he'd pick the girl for the activity, not the other way around. He liked to go to the stock-car races and fishing, not just the movies or a party.

And he never had a problem getting a date if he wanted one. All sorts of girls liked him, and I knew it wasn't just for his looks. I had dark eyes and brown hair too, though I kept mine shorter so it wouldn't hang in my face when I ran. But I've had girls turn me down; if he did, he never said.

Well, no matter why the heart had gone out of my relationship with Amy, it was gone, and I wouldn't be letting myself get locked in again anytime too soon.

Berry's mom and younger sister, Deena, were at the end of the driveway tying a scarecrow to the side of the mailbox. When I got out, they yelled to me to go on in.

Berry was drying dishes, the sleeves of a ragged NASA sweatshirt pushed up to her elbows.

"Hi, Jeff. Go on back to my room. There's all kinds of books in there."

"I'll wait," I said, leaning against the counter. She was a full head shorter than me and I stared down at her. It must have made her uncomfortable.

"Come on, I'm done." She threw the towel down and headed toward her room.

She pointed at the shelves and I knelt down to look.

"Berry, I need to see something about dreams."

"What about them? I don't have any of those interpretation books if that's what—"

"No. I don't need to find out what something means. I just want to know why. I've had a couple of weird dreams."

I heard her sit on the bed. "Did you dream about Mike?"

Man! Spooky. I turned and sat on the floor. Leaning back against the shelves, I looked at her, then around the room. It was like going back in time. Her walls were still decorated with rock posters and star charts. Her one doll, a Raggedy Ann nearly as old as Berry herself, sat by the pillow.

It was like before, when we discovered we could talk about the Cop's Kid Syndrome. Together, alone in this room, we could listen to the laughter of parents and sisters down the hall and look at each other and say, "What if one of our dads got shot?"

It was something I said out loud only to her, and she to me, and we'd fix any damage done voicing it by repeating a word charm: "Words don't make it so." And they didn't, here in this room. Somehow, here, it was acceptable and understood.

"Did you, Jeff? Did you dream about Mike?"

I nodded. "Twice." Maybe it was the room that made me want to tell her everything. "Berry, what if . . . ?"

"What if what?" she asked quietly, going prone on her elbows, her face toward me.

"What if something happened to him? Something bad."

With a sigh she put her face to the mattress, and her arms straightened, hands dangling over the edge. "Maybe you'd better tell me about the dreams."

"I had the same dream, on two different nights."

I studied her fingers and told her what happened in the dream, how he looked, what was said. When I was done, she sat up to turn the bed lamp on. I hadn't noticed it was getting dark.

"Move it over," she said, and came to kneel beside me, facing the shelves. "There's different kinds of dreams, you know. They work out problems while you sleep by using symbols that your subconscious can understand. You could be dealing with your worry over Mike, but it's strange that you've had the dream twice, exactly the same."

She pulled out a book with *ESP* in its title and opened it on her lap. "Then there are dreams that tell the future. Prophetic dreams are sometimes recurrent."

"Well . . . ," I said as she flipped through the pages.

"I'm not saying it *is* a prophetic dream. The examples in this book aren't the greatest, but they're the only ones I've got to show you." She tapped a finger on the page. "Did you ever hear of Maria Marten and the murder at the red barn?"

"No." I looked at the woodcut print of a screaming female, her hair blowing backward.

"It was in London, in 1828. Maria Marten was found dead and buried in the barn after her mother had a dream about it."

"You're right. That's not a great example."

She sighed. "But, Jeff, that's the only kind of dream you'll find in these books, those that have a tragedy related to them."

"Like death."

"Right. But that doesn't mean you can't have a dream about a dog wearing a bow tie every night for a week. You're probably working out a lot of feelings about Mike."

"But this was different! I knew I was dreaming. I knew I could find him and ask him questions, and I did."

"That's lucid dreaming." She shut the book and pulled another from the shelf.

"What?" I watched her flip through the pages.

"Here. 'Lucid dreaming,' " she read aloud, " 'is when the dreamer is aware he is in a dream, thereby gaining some measure of control over it, unlike other dreams where he is not only in them but of them.' Understand?" She tossed the book at me. "There's a couple of chapters in there about dreaming and lucid dreaming."

"Thanks." I saw how she lowered her eyes and picked at the laces on her shoes. "You don't think . . . ? Never mind." I'd wanted to ask her if she thought the dreams could be real, if Mike really was asking me to come get him. It sounded crazy.

"Okay. Well, read that and if it's not what you wanted to know, just tell me."

"Can I borrow the other one too?"

She handed it to me. "This is weird, Jeff. You asking me all this."

"I don't know anybody else who knows about this stuff."

"You mean you don't know anyone else who's weird like me, huh?"

"No! I—"

"The scarecrow's up!" Deena burst into the room. "You said we could do the jack-o'-lantern after dark."

Berry and I stood up at the same time, almost cracking skulls. Berry laughed. "You want to help carve?"

"I really ought to go."

Blink. The smile on her face went off fast.

"Okay." She tapped the books with a finger. "Let me know if you need something else."

"Tell me something, Berry. Do I tell Kirby or not?"

"That's your call, Jeff. If you don't feel right about it, don't. Maybe you'll have another one."

"And what if I don't tell him and . . ." I looked at eight-year-old Deena.

"Hey, Deena," Berry said. "Go get us some newspaper and take it out back to the picnic table. Take the pumpkin out, but don't touch any knives! I'll be out in a minute."

" 'Kay. Bye, Jeff."

Deena ran out. I felt Berry's hand on my arm. "You act like you believe it really *was* a message from Mike."

I looked at the hand, watched it drop away. "I don't know."

"Oh, Jeff." My name came out on a soft breath.

I met her eyes. "I know what you're thinking."

"No you don't." The corners of her mouth went up in a halfhearted smile.

"It's okay," I said. "Remember our old rules: Just like words, dreams don't make it so."

"Dreams don't make it so," she echoed. Then she turned off her bed lamp and I followed her out of the room.

I was reading one of the books when Dad came into the den. He sat down in the chair across from me, so I looked at him.

"Will you be passing flyers out this weekend?" he asked.

"I did it the last two weekends," I said, rubbing my eyes, covering my embarrassment. I'd helped Mike's parents with the Missing Person flyers until I felt I could drop. The work didn't bother me, it was Mr. and Mrs. Thayer.

"You haven't been to see them all week," he said.

"It's hard, Dad. Every time Mrs. Thayer looks at me it's like she's begging me to tell her I know where he is. It's like she's saying, 'You're his best friend; you know something you're not telling.' "

Dad stretched his legs out. "I can't tell you that I know what you're going through. I can try to imagine, but that's as close as I can get. I just ask that you try to put your feelings aside when you look at Mike's parents. Try to imagine what they feel, what they're going through, and to what lengths they'd go to find one piece of solid information. Will you do that?"

"Yes. But sometimes, Dad, it's hard, because I get scared about him being gone. I don't want them to see that."

"I know," he said slowly. "This is especially hard for you because you see a lot of things differently than other kids. You *know* the statistics on runaways and missing children from hearing me talk about them at home. I never realized it would become real to you, to us. And I'm sorry."

"Like it's your fault you wanted us aware of things," I said with a laugh.

He nodded and we sat quietly for a while. "Dad," I said, "you should hear the rumors around school." I told him a few of the choicest ones, like the one where Mike was hiding out for a Halloween prank. It was too ridiculous for words.

"We got a lot of calls coming into the station too. Well-meaning people have reported seeing him on every road in and out of town. We're steadily running down every lead. When he gets home, we'll have to tell him."

That was lame for Dad, I thought. But I loved him for saying it. "Dad, you'd tell me if you got something solid, wouldn't you?"

"You know that depends, Jeff."

"The pig story," I said with a sigh.

"That's the one."

"Dad, I don't think the pig story applies here."

"The pig story nearly always applies, Jeff."

"Dad, Mike disappearing is not a stolen-pig story." The instant it was out of my mouth I realized I could be very wrong.

"The pig story nearly always applies," he repeated.

"Not if Mike ran away," I said, suddenly desperate.

"I understand what you're getting at, Jeff, but if he ran away, then he's the one who took the pig."

I sighed. "You win, Dad." There was no fighting that pig.

Chapter 3

There was a farmer who raised the finest hogs in the county. But his prize hog, his sow, was his bacon, so to speak. It had countless litters and put many a dollar in the farmer's pocket. One morning in early winter, the farmer found that his hog was gone. Tire tracks and a trail of crumbled biscuits told the farmer that she'd been stolen, probably for butchering.

Instead of raising a ruckus, he kept the theft to himself. It was ten months later when, at the county fair, a man he'd known a long time walked up to him and cast an appraising eye over his stock. The farmer greeted him and they exchanged small talk. Then the man asked him, "Say, did you ever find out who made off with that pig of yours?"

The farmer smiled.

I've heard the pig story all my life, it seems. Dad used it to explain why information was kept from the public in any kind of criminal case. It was along the same lines as giving a man enough rope to hang himself. Dad said that the pig story nearly always applies to cases, and I tried to tie it to Mike and me but couldn't. I didn't see how giving me information, if there was any, would harm the search for Mike. I certainly didn't steal the pig. But I was only the cop's kid and I had to go along with the cop.

I read the books Berry gave me, and as if going to her had jinxed it, I didn't have the dream again. I wrote down every detail in a notebook so I wouldn't miss anything, in case I needed to remember it later. The only thing the books did was make me wonder more.

Besides the red barn thing, there were other dreams cited where murders were solved or important documents found. These dreams had direct results from the messages. But the messages came from dead people.

Mike had sent a message, if it was real.

If it wasn't just a dream.

Leaves in his hair.

His clothes damp.

"Get Kirby and come get me."

"Hey, Kirby." I walked up his driveway and kicked the tire of his red truck. He slid out from beneath it. Grease covered his fingers and he looked up at me with surprise in his clear blue eyes.

"Jeff, whatcha up to?"

"Nothing. I stopped by the station and your dad said you were at home, so I thought I'd come by. Saw the garage light."

He didn't answer, just kept watching my face.

I shrugged. "I was bored."

He got up and wiped his hands on the sides of his coveralls, then swept the kerchief off his blond head. "You? Bored on a Saturday night? Like I've been saying for ages, Jeff, you gotta get a real job."

I laughed and waved it away. I'd worked for the same landscaper for the past three summers. Kirby had always made wisecracks about it, saying he hadn't had a day off since he could walk.

But where he had a dad who could pull him into a business, I had a dad who believed school years should be spent on getting the best grades possible. At least that's what he said. I thought it had more to do with his fear of what could happen to somebody in charge of a cash register. He'd seen too many shaken or hurt kids who'd had to face a punk with a gun.

I followed Kirby to the workbench, where he put the wrench into a drawer of his toolbox. "You too wrapped up here to ride somewhere with me?"

"Like where? I was only changing the oil. I'm about done."

"I don't know. We could go bowling, talk."

"Ugh! You *must* be bored!"

I wondered why I'd thought I could tell him. "I was helping Mike's folks today with flyers and all. It's tough."

He looked away. "I can imagine. They must be going crazy."

"They are. I am too."

His eyes met mine for a second, then went to the truck. I was used to the discomfort I caused in people by bringing Mike's name into the conversation.

He nudged me aside, went to the driver's door, and got in. "Let me write the mileage down," he said as he reached up to the visor. "You should always write your mileage down when you change your oil." He said it like he was teaching me something. I looked in through the passenger-side window as he pulled a notepad down. He reached for the glove compartment and opened it. "Where's a pen?"

His greasy hand dived inside and sent a map falling to the floor. I opened the door and bent to get the map. "Thanks," he said.

I saw him draw the pen out, its end caught in a length of narrow brown ribbon. "You got a tape unwound, huh?"

"Tape?" He shook it off, and without waiting for me to replace the map, he shut the glove box. "Oh, yeah," he said, scratching his head with the pen before writing down the mileage. "The damn player in here eats tapes."

"Oh."

He looked at me and took the map from my hand.

"You know, I ought to straighten up around here, then get a shower. If you don't mind I'll skip riding out with you. If you wanna stay, you can. Grab that broom over there."

I watched him put the notepad and pen above the visor. "It's okay. I was kind of hoping we could talk, but it's not important. Only . . ." *Only talk about finding Mike! Only talk about these crazy dreams where he wants us to come get him!*

"Talk while I work."

"Nah. It was dumb, anyway. I just had some dreams about Mike, that's all." I closed the door and stepped away, feeling stupid. How could anyone understand the urgency I felt over the dreams?

"Dreams are funny, that's for sure." I heard the door slam and his boots on the concrete floor as he rounded the front of the truck. "Makes you wonder who has more fun, you or your dream-self."

"Yeah," I said. There was no way I could tell him we had to go get Mike. Not now. The moment had passed. "Well, look, Kirby, I'll just see you later."

"Okay, sure, take it easy." He looked half puzzled, half relieved as I walked out.

Man, you are so dumb, I told myself. How could I come to Kirby with this crazy, awful dream and expect him to understand it? He'd laugh me out of there. He probably spends his dream life in the *Sports Illustrated* swimsuit issue.

That's what I kept telling myself as I drove to Berry's house: It was just a dream. She looked as surprised as Kirby had been when I showed up. She took the books from me.

"You read all this?"

"The parts about dreams, yeah. I stayed up two nights reading." I laughed a little. "Maybe that's why I haven't dreamed it again. I read myself to sleep."

"Any questions?"

"One. You want to go bowling?"

When we entered the alley, all except one duckpin lane were taken. We got sodas and some fries and sat down to wait for a lane. "I went to see Kirby," I said.

"What did he say?"

"Nothing really. I didn't tell him. I was going to," I added, "but at the last minute it didn't feel right."

"What do you mean?"

"Well, he seemed uncomfortable when I brought Mike's name up. When I said something about dreams he told me how funny dreams are. It made me back off."

Berry nodded and ate some fries.

"Have you ever done that lucid dreaming stuff?" I asked her.

She shook her head. "No. I understand it, at least I think I do, but I don't recall ever being aware that I was dreaming."

"That one book makes it sound like I could change the dream if it happened again. Do you believe that?"

"They say you can. How would you change it?"

"I'd try to ask him different questions."

"Like what?"

"Like, 'Is this just a dream, or are you really telling me something?' "

"What if he doesn't answer the new questions?"

"Then it would mean it was just a dream. So in a way, I'd get the answer."

"Ask him what he lost."

"What?"

"Remember? He said he lost something. Ask him about it. Hey, that lane is free."

We had started our game and Berry was already ahead two strikes to a spare when I realized how I was filling in time, wasting it. A hot rush of guilt passed over me as I thought of Mike waiting for me . . . if he was. If it was real and he was waiting, I shouldn't be bowling. I should be looking for him. But where?

Just as I was making my approach, I heard a girl's voice a few lanes down from us. I let go of the ball. It sounded like Amy. It had to be her.

"Are you sure?" the girl was saying. "I never did this before."

I bowled a spare and walked back to Berry. "I'm not doing very well." She marked the score.

"Amy's here," Berry said as she got up to let me sit down.

"Must be a twin," I answered without looking. "She hates bowling."

When I felt Berry's eyes leave my face, I looked down two lanes to see who Amy was with. Craig Hoffman. Basketball forward. Not bad, Amy, I thought.

On the way home, after I'd been severely beaten by Berry, she asked, "Did you and Amy break up, or are you taking time out?"

I shrugged. "I have no idea."

"No idea? She didn't seem like she was sneaking behind your back. She even waved to us."

"I mean we haven't talked about breaking up. It's just that the other day we looked at each other and sighed, you know? And so . . . now she likes to bowl."

Berry laughed a little. "So here you are, no Mike to talk to, no Amy to talk to, and you're stuck with good ol' Berry."

I laughed with her. "Us cops' kids gotta stick together. Besides, it's not like I'm hurt or anything. I even told Mike I wasn't as comfortable with Amy as I used to be."

"You miss him more than you let on," she said.

I could feel her watching my face in the dark car. All of a sudden I was angry. "Let on? What do you want me to do, Berry? Are you waiting for me to pull the car over and break down into sobs or something? You want some drama?"

"No! But you need to do something! Passing flyers out helps his folks more than it does you. Maybe you should do something for yourself, something that can make you feel better."

"Like what?" I'd do anything.

"Have you stopped by his church? He's Catholic, and Catholics light candles for prayers. I went in the other evening and lit one for him. It made me feel better."

"You did?" She hardly knew Mike. "Why did you do that?"

"Because of him. Because of you."

Her voice was small in the car. The anger let go of me and I wanted to kick myself for hurting Berry's feelings. She had been right on the money when she'd said I wasn't letting on, that I needed to do something for myself. I wanted to apologize but didn't know how.

I didn't speak again until I dropped her off at her house. "That's nice, what you did for Mike."

"Try it," she said before swinging the door shut.

I watched her as she went up to the house and got safely inside. So—I should light a candle for Mike so *I* could feel better?

And what would Mike think? I thought about the crucifix in the Thayers' living room, the statue of Mary in the flower bed. How much had Mike bought into all that? I just didn't know. But after all these years, the question had become important to me.

Chapter 4

Trick-or-treaters are a determined lot.

They come in darkness, in cold and wind, under rainy or star-masked skies. They come in hopes of one more candy bar, one more pack of gum. This year they came in spite of a chilly breeze and a missing Mike. But they came in groups.

I handed out the chocolate kisses and cherry licorice to the imps and ghosts, counting the number of superheroes in each batch. Dad had taken my sister, Katy, now six, to do her rounds. She was in her third annual princess costume, but Mom said all girls go through a long princess phase.

At this moment, no doubt, Amy and her date were getting ready for the Halloween party at Chad Maybrick's house. I would have been costumed, keys in hand, anxious to be on time so I wouldn't break Amy's cardinal rule number two: Thou shalt not be late. It was just as well I didn't know who her date was. I'd be sorely tempted to call him up and stall him.

Not that I was jealous, mind you. It was more like wanting to teach him how to swim by throwing him into the deep end.

For a few minutes I regretted not going. Amy had been planning pirate costumes for us. I wondered what she'd look like all got up as a pirate's wench. I usually enjoyed myself at parties, and it seemed like a long time since I'd been to one. Maybe music, low lights, and warm bodies would have done me good. But I knew I'd still feel alone.

I looked into the eyes of each trick-or-treater, when I could see them, but I didn't recognize any of Mike's brothers or sisters. I wondered if the Thayers were keeping them in. I felt bad for the kids, if that was the case. Between doorbell rings I dialed Mike's number.

The oldest girl answered. "Hey," I said. "This is Jeff. Did you guys go trick-or-treating already?"

"Hi, Jeff. Nope. We were going to go to the fire hall, but Mom's got a headache."

The fire hall had a party every year and all the trick-or-treaters ended up there. Loose candy, and penny boxes for saving and donating back to the hall, were handed out at the door, and punch and cookies were served to everybody. This event had been held for the past fifty years or so, and every kid in town could show you right off the bat which engine the pennies had helped buy.

"That's too bad," I said. "Listen, why don't you guys sit tight, and I'll come get you. We can still make it for the costume judging and all."

"Really, Jeff?"

"Really, Theresa." I saw her eleven-year-old face, freckled and pink. "You go tell your mom that I'll be there to pick you up in twenty minutes or so. Help everybody get ready, will you?"

"You bet!"

After hanging up, I told Mom she had door duty, and I left. Visions of goblins dashing under the back wheels of the car made me extra cautious as I backed out of the driveway. This was something I could do for Mike. For me.

There's nothing quite like having five kids in your car, all excited about going to a party. Unless it's bringing those same kids home again, full of sugar.

"Let's go by the haunted barn!" one of them yelled above the rest as we left the fire hall. I thought it was Philip.

"Yeah!"

"Oh, pleeeease, Jeff!"

"Scary!"

"All right, all right! Hold it down!" I yelled louder than them. When it got quiet I slowed the car. "You want me to drive up that scary road and . . . and go by the haunted barn?" I asked, mock fear in my voice, and the two girls giggled.

"Jeff's scared!" the boys yelled.

"Aren't you?" I asked.

"No!" they all screamed.

"What do you think, Theresa?" She was up front with me.

Everybody remained quiet, awaiting her reply. Except for Frank, the oldest boy. He whispered, "Say yes. Say yes."

"Okay, Jeff," Theresa said. I could tell she was pleased, both by the cheering that met her answer and by the fact that I'd asked her opinion.

The haunted barn, as they called it, was a foundation of big stones, the remainder of a bank barn, part of an old farm. Most of the acreage had been parceled out to house lots, but the foundation of the barn remained on untouched land that fronted a large woods. There were stories of the barn, as it had been, appearing out of the mists to travelers on rainy nights, who felt compelled to head into it for shelter. When they came out, grateful and dry, they would look back to see: no barn.

There was no telling the kids that the whole story was ridiculous, not only for the obvious reason that travelers don't need to seek shelter in barns in this day and age, but also because there are no travelers around these parts.

The road that led up to the barn was paved now, but I remember when it was graveled and rutted. Trees grow thick on either side until you get to the houses. I had always known it as Shivers Lane.

"Lock your doors!" I told them as we turned onto Shivers Lane. They laughed and I felt good. When I was younger I liked having goose bumps from spooky things. It was a fun-scared thrill they were after.

I slowed the car again as we neared the barn. "I sure wouldn't want to live up here," I muttered.

Beside me, Theresa reached for her throat. I did a double take. "Theresa? Are you okay?"

She nodded, eyes wide, and I saw her fist wrap around a white ribbon, which she'd pulled from beneath her costume. She stared ahead, gripping it.

"What's that?"

"Huh? Oh," she said, opening her palm. "It's just my scapular."

I didn't know what a scapular was, but it seemed to be a charm of some sort for her.

"Oh no," I mumbled. "I think I'm almost out of gas." With perfect timing, I pulled off to the side of the road, abreast of the barn, and cutting the engine, rolled to a stop.

"You're not out of gas *really*, are you, Jeff?" Frank's laugh was forced.

"Hard to tell. My gas gauge is stuck." I hid my smile. I

knew some would say it was tormenting them, but I wouldn't have done it if I hadn't known they'd be talking about it for weeks.

"Come on, Jeff," Jimmy pleaded. "You're trying to scare us."

"Me!" I hit the steering wheel with my palm. "You guys are the ones who wanted to come here." I turned to look back at them. All four were sitting, eyes front, pressing hands against their nervous giggles. Theresa bravely pushed her nose against the glass, staring at the dark mound of the foundation.

"Frank," I pleaded. "Get out and see if my gas cap fell off."

"No way!" he hollered.

I laughed and turned the dome light on, making them all squint. "Do you think the ghosts can see us better now?"

In the backseat they climbed over each other to take turns cupping their hands and peering out the window. Even Marie gave it a peek.

Philip stuck his tongue out at the window. "Take that, you old ghosts!" We applauded his bravery and I looked at Theresa. She wasn't laughing with the rest of us. She'd let her scapular drop to her chest. It was a picture on fabric, encased in plastic, not much larger than a postage stamp, of the Virgin Mary holding something out to a kneeling monk.

"Jeff?" The picture was covered by her fist again. "I told Mom we wouldn't be late."

"Oh, okay. Well, you guys," I said, letting the car go dark again. "If somebody gives me a stale old piece of candy, I might get this old banger to run on fumes."

A piece of taffy was handed up to me and I chewed it thoughtfully before starting the car. Heading back down Shivers Lane, I shook my head. "I don't know, you guys. That candy's pretty bad. Maybe you'd better give it all over to me."

"No way!" Frank said. "You're not fooling us."

At their house, the backseat emptied fast. Theresa was closing her door as I moved to follow the others into the house. I hung back, waiting for Theresa.

"You okay?" I asked. Maybe I'd really frightened her. "I hope you had a good time."

"I did." She looked up at me. "When we first pulled up, I thought I saw something at the barn, that's all."

Don't tease her, I warned myself. "Like what?"

"Something . . . somebody." She waved a hand in the air and went past me to the door. "It was probably a reflection on the window, from the light."

Inside, Mrs. Thayer was being treated to an account of the party and adventure. The kids worked a kind of magic on her. She smiled, then grinned, then laughed with them.

"Jeff, thank you so much for taking them. I couldn't."

"Hey, it's no biggie. I wanted some company."

"Jeff took us to the haunted barn, Mommy," Marie whispered. "And he ran out of gas." She nodded grimly.

"My goodness!" Mrs. Thayer clasped her hands over her mouth.

"We weren't afraid," Frank told her.

"Only of the gas cap," Marie finished.

Mrs. Thayer smiled and kissed Marie's forehead. "Aren't you all brave? Now, go clean off the makeup. I want to speak with Jeff."

I watched them run from the room, dreading meeting Mrs. Thayer's eyes. But when I did, I didn't feel the stab of uneasiness and guilt I'd expected.

Instead, I felt drawn into them with a warmth. I froze as she crossed the space to me, and still didn't move as her eyes teared and her arms came up around my neck.

"Thank you, Jeff," she whispered. "I'd hoped . . ."

She didn't have to finish her thought. She'd hoped Mike could be here to take the kids out tonight. Suddenly I wrapped her in my arms. Here was a safe place to cry, I told myself. And burying my face between her shoulder and cheek, I almost did. I really wanted to.

We stood for several moments like that, until the door behind me opened and we drew apart.

"Michael." Mike's mother wiped her cheeks and smiled at her husband. "You look bushed." He was on the maintenance crew at the hospital.

He threw his jacket on the sofa and slapped my shoulder. "How're you doing, Jeff?"

"I'm okay," I answered, knowing he wouldn't need the whole truth. "I guess you want to get into the driveway, don't you?"

"I parked on the street. You don't have to rush out because of that."

"I should go anyway."

"Okay. I'll walk out with you, then."

I turned to say good-bye to Mrs. Thayer, but she'd already left the room. Once outside, I breathed deeply, feeling my head clear.

"I took the kids to the fire hall," I said.

"I was going to, but the boiler started making a racket."

I laughed. I knew the stories of the hospital's possessed boiler as well as any Thayer. "Next budget meeting, huh?"

"Yup."

Another slap on my shoulder to dismiss me, and I got in the car. As I waved good-bye to him I couldn't help agreeing with his wife. Mr. Thayer did look bushed. Worn and harried.

Halfway home, I passed the fire hall and thought of the kids and how Mike would have had fun taking them to the haunted barn himself. Theresa's apparition was something Berry would love to hear about.

The smile froze as my whole face went numb. Theresa had seen something when we first pulled up, she'd said. Probably a reflection from the light, she'd said.

I hadn't turned on the dome light until after the teasing over the gas tank being empty. The whole backseat had been peering out the window at that time, but no one else had said they saw something.

Theresa must have been mistaken about the time.

Or, there were kids up there daring each other on Halloween night. It had to be one of those explanations. I toyed with the idea of running back up there, checking it out for myself.

No. It would be better done in daylight.

The next day I drove up to the barn just before dark. Brown grass rustled under my feet as I walked far enough up the slope to see the foundation, littered with trash and weeds. Ghosts don't leave trash.

There is no such thing as ghosts.

Berry can say what she wants.

Theresa can see what she wants. She can claim the adventure for years, tell her grandchildren about the haunted barn and the figure that might have been a reflection.

I, for one, didn't believe in ghosts.

And that's what I was telling myself when I got the feeling that something just wasn't right up there. I couldn't explain it and didn't hang around to try.

Chapter 5

I was calling Mike's name as I ran. Excitement preceded me down the tilted hallway and led me around each corner.

Mike leaned nonchalantly on a locker with a crooked grin on his shadow-split face. "You gotta learn to relax, man," he said.

Stopping a mere two feet from him, I caught my breath. "You look pretty relaxed," I said.

He shrugged. "Got nothing else to do."

"I tried to talk to Kirby like you wanted, Mike."

He nodded. "It's okay. You found it, that's all that matters. You found it and you'll know."

"I don't understand. Where are you? Why don't you come home?"

Mike pushed himself away from the locker and banged it with his fist. His face hardened in an expression I'd never seen on him before.

"Help me out, will ya?" he yelled.

"You know I will!" I yelled as loudly as he had. "I want to, but I can't understand any of this! Is this real?"

Mike's face went slack and he sighed. The low, rumbling chuckle that came from him drew me up straight. "Oh, man," he said. "This is too freaking real."

"Great! Now tell me exactly how to help. *Please*."

"Think, Jeff. You've gotta do the thinking, because my head hurts . . . so bad." He ran a hand over his head and leaned against the locker.

Think. Think.

This is lucid dreaming.

I'm in control. Ask him specific questions.

"Mike, I need to ask you something."

"No. I'm tired. I'm gonna go lie down. I'll wait for you to come get me."

"Where?" I watched him begin to move away from me like before, only slower. I tried, but I couldn't move after him. His grin came back and he lifted his hand in a wave.

I sat up, shaking in a cold sweat. It was two-fifteen. The same time I'd awakened from the other dream.

I got out of bed and went to the kitchen for a soda, wishing I could call Berry. I knew I'd never get back to sleep after the dream, so I went back to my room and sat down to write the whole thing out, under the dream I'd set down before.

I hadn't seen Berry to talk to since I'd yelled at her

in the car after our bowling game. I still hadn't apologized.

Well, I was going to talk to her today. I *had* to.

My hand shook as I dated the dream November seventh.

When I got to the last part, the most horrible part of the dream, I tried to write it exactly the way it had occurred, but without feeling, without the fear that wrapped itself around my insides.

He said his head hurt, and rubbed his hand over it. He said he was tired and was going to lie down and wait for me to come get him. He wouldn't answer my question. He moved backward, down the hall, slowly and with a grin. He waved.

He waved with the hand that had rubbed his aching head.

Its palm was smeared with blood.

Throwing the pen down, I took a shaky breath and picked up the can of soda. As I lifted it to my mouth, a drop of icy sweat dripped from it to my naked thigh. The shock of it made my heart thud hard and I wondered how long a heart could stand being gripped by fear.

Turning off my desk lamp, I pulled the cold can gratefully to my chest and, pressing it there, listened for my heartbeat in the dark.

At lunch I headed over to Berry's table with my tray. Molly wasn't there, just Berry at one end, all by her lonesome. She looked up when I slid the tray against hers.

"I figured you'd sit with me today," she said.

"Yeah, you're psychic, right?" I eased my legs under the table and sat down beside her.

She snorted daintily. "Hardly," she said. "See who's in your seat?"

I looked over at the table where I'd been sitting with a couple of guys the last week or so. Amy was ensconced between two burly jocks.

"She misses me, Berry." I opened the carton of milk and took a swig.

"She does, huh?"

"Yup," I said, feeling one of our old sarcasm battles coming on. I sighed. "She misses me pret-ty bad."

Berry's bottom lip quivered as she tried not to smile. "That's really sad. Now she's compensating with them."

"I guess I'm a lot of man to replace."

She nodded gravely. "Craig didn't have a chance."

I laughed first and then she was laughing with me.

I rocked my shoulder against hers. "You're good," I said.

She smiled. "So, how are you?"

"Fine, I guess." Tell her about the dream, I ordered myself. "You?"

"Okay. Carrion complimented me on my driving this morning. He said I was a natural behind the wheel."

"Good," I said with a laugh. Carrion was the nickname given to Mr. Carone, the driver's ed. teacher, years ago because he loved showing the accident movies to his classes. "Think he's heard the myth about cops' kids shoplifting and driving without a license?"

She laughed. My words took me back.

"Let's go, let's go!" I remembered Mike saying from the backseat of my grandfather's car. We were fifteen and my grandfather was making a pharmacy stop before dropping us off at the swimming pool.

"C'mon, Jeff!" Mike said, and before I thought about it, we were going around the strip mall's parking lot. By the time we'd circled the lot for the fifth time, my grandfather was watching us from the sidewalk. I pulled to the curb and slid over into the passenger seat, embarrassed, waiting for a setdown.

"You got done fast, Mr. Owens," Mike said.

My grandfather hadn't said a word to us, and if he said anything to my father, I never heard.

I came out of the reverie and stared at my lunch.

"I had a dream," I blurted out, surprising myself.

"Another one? What happened?"

I leaned closer to her, feeling the flutter in my chest. My tongue had gone dry. "I think he's dead."

She paled. "Jeff!"

Letting the words up through my vocal chords had been a mistake. I felt sick, and swallowing frantically, I stood up from the table. Trying to act normal, I headed toward the doors that led outside to the back fields.

Outside, I breathed in the cool air, feeling it go down to the very bottom of my lungs. When I exhaled, I heard a strange whimpering noise. I walked straight ahead, until the buildings no longer showed muddy red in the corner of my eye and there was only the sound of my heart in my ears.

I stopped and took another deep breath. Exhaling produced the same whimper, and I knew for certain it was me. I felt my face, found it dry. In a way, that was a letdown. Slowly I became aware of something else.

Someone stood behind me. Quietly. Patiently. Berry had followed me. I was glad for it. I felt my hand reach backward.

When she didn't take my hand I turned.

There was no one there.

Chapter 6

Across from me Berry slurped noisily at her milk shake.

"This is the best," she said. She wiped her mouth with a napkin and sat back with a sigh. "Thanks for the shake."

" 'Sokay." I looked out the big plate-glass window beside me. Railroad tracks ran between the road and the end of the diner. Sometimes, if you turned your face fully to the windows as a train passed, you could fool your body into thinking it was moving the other way.

One humid night in August Mike and I had come to the diner for his favorite cheesecake, after his shift taking tickets at the Majestic. A westbound train came by; its lights seemed to waver and its blasting diesel whistle warbled in the heavy air. Mike pressed his face to the glass.

"We're heading east, man," he said.

"Are we?"

"Yeah. Trains on parallel tracks, passing in the night."

I played along, feeling the movement until the train was gone. "We've stopped."

Mike looked at me and grinned. "Home again."

"Big deal," I said. I was ready to head for greener pastures. "This time next year I'll be heading for college and you might be in boot camp. Can you believe it?"

Mike shrugged. "I can't even think about it now. Ask me in the spring."

That's Mike, I had thought at the time. Where I was always lost without having a master plan worked out in front of me, Mike seemed to have things fall into place without trying. Either he very quietly sweated things out, or he was charmed.

Not so charmed, I thought now as I looked out into the night. Across the road, on the other side of the diner, was the Majestic. Mike had worked there Saturdays and two or three other nights a week since his sixteenth birthday.

"Jeff," Berry said.

"Huh?"

"You okay?"

"Yeah, I'm fine."

I'd told Berry the whole dream, bloody hand and all, after I'd picked her up at her house.

Now she said, "I wanted to follow you out of the cafeteria today, but I was afraid to."

"Afraid?" I laughed under my breath. "I thought you had."

"You did?"

I nodded but I didn't know how to tell her I'd sensed someone behind me and that it must have been Mike.

"I've been waiting for you to give me your opinion, Berry."

"I don't know what to say. I believe you, that the dream was like you said. And that's what makes it so scary." She leaned forward. "I don't like to think this is a case for the books."

"You're saying it sounds like one."

"Yeah, I guess I am. But that doesn't mean it is."

"That doesn't make sense, Berry. Either it is or it isn't." I leaned forward to grab her hand and hissed through gritted teeth, "Don't you know that I'm going crazy with this stuff?"

"Yes!" she whispered just as harshly. "That's why I think you should go and talk to somebody."

"I am! I'm talking to you!"

She hesitated and forced herself to answer. "As far as I can see, all I've done is help feed your fears with those books. And I'm really sorry for that."

I squeezed her hand and was about to tell her it wasn't true when Kirby walked up to the booth. I let go of her and sat back.

"Hi," I said to him and Jenny Whitman, his off-again, on-again girlfriend. He pushed in beside me. Berry grudgingly slid over so Jenny, in her McDonald's uniform, could slide in too.

"What are you two up to?" Kirby asked.

"Nothing much."

"In a hurry to leave?"

"Well—"

"No." Berry butted in. "You just getting off work, Jenny?"

"Uh-huh." Jenny smiled sweetly to Berry with bright red lips and fluffed the bangs of her short-cropped blond hair with matching red nails. "Can I have that ashtray, please?"

As Jenny lit a cigarette Kirby said, "Saw your car, Jeff."

The waitress came to pour coffee and Kirby ordered.

"Seeing you two together's pretty funny," Kirby said.

"Why's that?"

"You know." He nudged me with his elbow. "You were whispering and I guess I connected it with Mike. I couldn't help wondering if the cops know anything."

I looked at Berry. "No, Kirby. We were just talking."

Jenny turned her attention to Berry. "Do I know you?"

"We're in the same English class."

"Oh, right," she said with a knowing look. Or maybe it was a smoker's squint.

Kirby nudged me. "Still having dreams?"

I just stared at him until Berry's foot hit mine. "Yeah, I am. But like you said, dreams are funny."

"Right. And who can blame you? You can't go anywhere without seeing his picture on a telephone pole. He's on the news, he's in the mall, he's at the damned gas station . . ." Kirby ran a hand through his hair and squirmed in the seat.

"Here we go again," Jenny said.

Kirby glared at her and lit a cigarette.

What had that been about? Kirby was digging a thumb into the corner of his eye, the lit end of the cigarette dangerously close to his hair.

"You'd been seeing a lot of Mike, hadn't you?" I asked him.

"About as much as I see you, except he came for parts every week," he said, fingers drumming the tabletop, "making a pest of himself."

"Pest?" I laughed a little.

"Always hanging around, sucking down a beer. A couple of times he told me he's praying for me." Kirby shot me a quick wide-eyed glance.

I rocked back. "You're kidding, right?"

"Come on!" he said in total disbelief. "He meant it. Gave me a saint's medal once."

I had to laugh. "I know he went to church and all."

"Maybe you never did anything that needed praying for, eh?"

When Kirby's food came, I drank my coffee while Berry talked to Jenny, and Kirby ate. I tried to remember

Mike saying he prayed for *anybody*, but couldn't. I knew he went to church, and that he was an altar boy, whatever that was. And he liked Kirby, said he hoped Kirby would end up doing more than running a gas station. But pray for him?

I watched Kirby from the corner of my eye.

If Kirby was full of it, what did he get out of saying it? If it was the truth . . . I was hurt. Religious beliefs are kind of personal, aren't they? Unless you're a televangelist or something. So why would Kirby know something that personal about Mike when I didn't know it? It didn't make me look like the best friend, the close-as-a-brother friend, that I thought I was.

I don't know why, but I turned to Kirby. I put my hand on his arm and forced his hand down. His fork clattered on the rim of the plate.

"What did you do that bothered him so much?"

"Who? Mike?"

The girls grew quiet and I felt Berry looking at me. "Yeah, Mike. Why would he make a point of telling you he was praying for you? What didn't he like?"

Kirby pulled his arm from under my hand. "I guess he saw problems with the way I live my life. You gonna take over for him now, is that it? You gonna light candles and pray to statues for me? Let me save you the trouble and tell you I don't want it."

"Okay, okay, I'm sorry. I just never knew, and—"

"Don't start bugging out, Jeff, but maybe there's a lot you don't know about Mike. You two weren't glued to each other. Did you ever think of that?"

The anger in his eyes made me blink. "No, I never did."

"Yeah, well, let's drop it, okay? This whole Mike thing is starting to freak everybody. I see him everywhere . . ." He picked up his fork.

Jenny's eyes were on her plate. Berry seemed sad, staring at the ashtray. I slid my foot across to nudge hers but she didn't look up. The red lights at the railroad crossing flashed. I looked out the window at the dark night, waiting for the train to pass.

When it came, I thought of that August night and Mike's parallel tracks. I looked at Berry's reflection. It was staring at mine. Our dark images locked dismal gazes and smiled blurry smiles.

We got up to leave. "I'll see you later, Kirby," I said.

"Yeah. And listen, come on by some night. We'll go bowling if we have to." He grinned like the old Kirby. I took it as a signal to forget what had passed at the table.

Berry was quiet until we got into the car and then she burst out, "You saw the way he looked at you. I thought he'd break your neck! So what if Mike prayed for him? And why on earth did you throw it at him like that? Good grief, Jeff!"

"Are you done?"

"Yes."

"Good."

"So what if Mike prayed for him?" she repeated.

I turned the ignition on. "So what? I didn't know it, that's so what!"

"Is that so bad?"

"Look, Berry, I know you're trying to understand the way I feel, but I honestly don't care if you do or not. Mike's one person, but Kirby seems to know a different version. None of this makes sense to me. Not the way he talked about Mike, and certainly not the way I feel about it."

And it was true. Why did I feel so bad? All of a sudden I felt left out, in the dark, not as close to Mike as Kirby was. Time to change the subject.

"You talked to Jenny for a long time."

"How long have those two been going together, do you know?"

"It's on and off. Must be on, right now. Why?" I turned left at the light and headed out of town.

"She has a mighty expensive ring on for a casual relationship, that's all. I saw that ring at Cooper's Jewelers in the summer. It cost a pretty penny."

"Maybe he didn't give it to her."

"She told me he did. What does he do to get that kind of money?"

"He works with his dad. I don't know if he gets paid or not. Why are you so curious?"

"I noticed a lot of weird stuff in her purse when she

dug her cigarettes out. Couple of sets of keys, little boxes and bags—one of which looked full of marijuana."

"Really?"

"I don't know what else."

Berry had the same drug education I had; it came with having fathers who are cops.

"I know Kirby fools with drugs, so why be surprised that his girlfriend does?"

"Maybe he does more than fool with them, Jeff."

I let that sink in. "Sell them, you mean?"

"He wouldn't be the only one around here, for pity's sake. I'm just saying it's possible."

"Berry, it wasn't Kirby's purse."

She gave me a scathing look. "It might explain Mike's concern for him."

"Hold it right there. Let me get used to the idea he spent time praying for someone, *with them knowing it*," I emphasized. "Then I'll start wondering why. Okay?"

"Okay!"

When I pulled into her driveway I put the car in park and turned in the seat to face her.

"What about the dream?"

She sighed heavily and crossed her arms. "If you're starting to believe one hundred percent that it's really Mike, then you should listen to him, to what he says. Think about it really hard. Try to figure out what you've already found, since he claims you've found something.

But don't obsess over it, okay?" The sad look came back on her face.

"Berry, why did you get so sad at the diner?"

"Because everything was getting so . . . dark. Kirby started mumbling about freaking out and you looked shell-shocked. It was awful."

"Do me a favor and make sure to tell me if we get too depressing for you."

"Jeff, don't attack me like that."

Before I could stop gaping like a fish, she was out of the car and running toward the house. I watched until she was safely inside.

Sooner or later Berry was going to quit letting these things slide and I was going to owe her a *huge* apology.

Driving home, I kept hearing Kirby say, "I see him everywhere." Berry had called it a dark scene. She was right. Kirby had been mumbling to himself, something Jenny had obviously seen before. It was almost like he was afraid. But what was he afraid of?

Chapter 7

The following Sunday I went to mass at Mike's church. I sat in the back and watched the regulars, who knew their parts. I gave up trying to find where we were in the book and always stood or knelt a second late. I tried to picture Mike responding to the prayers, answering the priest, and smiled at the fact that I couldn't see him without his ripped-knee jeans.

His brother Frank was the youngest of the altar boys and I thought of him at the haunted barn, how he'd been excited and fun. Different from the sober figure he was up there. At the front of the sanctuary long rows of candles flickered, and I wondered how many were burning for Mike. I left quietly just before communion, not wanting the Thayers to see me.

On Sundays Mike and I would sometimes get together and work on his car. Now that he was gone and I didn't have Amy to hang with either, I didn't know what to do with my day. I drove aimlessly, listening to music, until I figured I could do that at home in bed and headed there as a slow rain began to fall.

Everyone knows what's said about best-laid plans. When I entered the house I was met by my mother, a stricken look on her face.

"Jeff! I'm glad you're home. No one knew where you went."

For a second I thought she'd been afraid I'd disappeared too. "What's the matter?" I asked as I hung my jacket up. "I went over to Mike's church."

"I thought you'd heard it on the radio. They found a body, Jeff, but it can't be him. They say it's been out there for several months. It may be a girl."

Here I was, hardly in the door, and in a couple of sentences my mother had reduced me to a heap of jelly, then given me my legs back. I could feel the sweat popping out over my lip.

"Geez, Mom!" I swept past her and into the kitchen to grab a soda. I heard her following me.

"I'm sorry," she said. "I was just so afraid that you might have heard only part of it and thought the worst."

I leaned on the counter. How could I tell her that I was already thinking the worst? That one day it might be him they found. "I'm sorry I didn't tell anyone where I was going."

"How are Ellen and Michael? I haven't talked to them since Thursday."

"I didn't see them. Just Frank. I left before it was over."

She nodded. "It's all right. I'm going to call Ellen after supper."

I had started to walk away when she stopped me.

"Jeff, does it help to know that it's hard for me too? I try to put myself in their place, but I can't imagine what I'd do if you or Katy just disappeared. It even makes me feel guilty sometimes, thinking that when Michael and Ellen look at me they must see my children, at home, safe."

"Why is that, Mom? Why do we feel guilty?"

She hugged me and patted my chest. "Who knows? It must be because we love Mike. And there's nothing we can do to make it better."

I bit my lip and swallowed the lump that had formed in my throat as her eyes filled. She went to the pantry door, opened it, and stood there like she'd forgotten what she went for.

"What are we having for dinner tonight?" I asked, making it normal between us again.

"I don't know," she said with a sniff. "Do you have plans?"

"No. Look, I'm going to my room."

She nodded. I grabbed the portable phone and went down the hall.

I peeked in Katy's doorway when I heard her humming. She was sitting on her bed, dressing a doll. Her legs were buried under an assortment of miniature clothes and the pillowcase that held the remains of her Halloween stash.

"Hey, Katy."

"Hi."

"What are you doing?"

She shook the doll at me and rolled her eyes. "I'm playing."

"Just asking." I walked away smiling. Katy had the ability to make me feel dumb without trying. Come to think of it, most girls had that ability.

The first thing I did was shed my sweater and canvas jeans for a tee and sweatpants.

Mom's tears had only temporarily distracted me. A body had been found. I switched on an AM station that ran constant news and dialed Berry's number.

"Hel-lo!"

"Berry," I said.

"Jeff?"

"Did you hear?"

"Yes, and it scared me to death at first. You too?"

"Yeah. I almost pissed myself before my mom finished her story. I've got the radio on now."

"Some guys were out looking for a place to build a deer stand early this morning," she said.

"It's almost that time." I didn't have to finish the

thought. Berry knew as well as anybody that when deer season opened, some hunter would bag more than he bargained for. It was a rare year that went by without a body being found by hunters somewhere in the state. Dad said the police counted on it.

"What if it's that girl we heard so much about last year?"

"Didn't her parents say she might have run away?"

"I think so. But it's strange, isn't it? I mean, if it is her, then they might have to look at Mike's case again. The two lived within a twenty-mile radius—"

"They haven't stopped looking at Mike's case, and besides, this was a girl, not a guy."

"Jeff, you know what I mean. We won't know until they identify her body, anyway."

"Right." I was thinking: Could there be a connection?

"So are you going to sit and listen to the radio all day?"

"Maybe. What are you doing?"

"Nothing," she said. "I'm bored. Why don't you dress for the track? Come pick me up and we'll go out to school and run in the rain. We'll have the track all to ourselves."

"And get pneumonia and have a *room* to ourselves."

"Yeah, what do you say?"

I looked at the radio, then out at the drizzle. "Ten minutes?"

— — —

I had to admit, running until the muscles in my legs burned felt terrific. Berry was slower but she was still running, and as I started to lag, I slowed my pace to hers, keeping her in front of me at a steady distance. Our feet slapped the wet track loudly as the misty rain washed the sweat off our faces.

Berry saw him a moment before I did. As we rounded the curve I saw her hesitate, stumble, then catch herself. By then I saw Kirby's red truck alongside the wire fence and almost plowed her down. We exchanged looks and walked over to it.

He rolled the window down and turned the blaring rock music down with it. "Are you nuts or something?" he asked us.

I grasped the wire and fell against it, panting. "What . . . are you doing h . . . ?"

". . . here?" Berry finished for me.

Kirby laughed and hit the steering wheel. "Cracked, that's what you are, both of you. I saw your car in the lot, that's all. I was going to tell you tomorrow, but now's okay."

"What?"

"Wow, a whole sentence," he said with a grin; then his face grew serious. "I got some hubcaps today, just what Mike wanted. I don't know what to do with 'em."

I knew that cars were important to Kirby, and Mike's car was important to Mike. They had a bond there. Mike would want those hubcaps.

I took a deep breath and said, "Hold on to them."

Kirby nodded. "Thought so."

"You been . . . ," Berry started, then gulped air. "You been listening to the radio, Kirby?"

"No. Not many stations play my music. Why?"

"They found a body today, but it isn't Mike." I said it in a rush and realized the job Mom had had, trying to get it out quickly, painlessly. Kirby rubbed a hand over his face and let his head fall back.

"Damn," he said. "Where?"

I looked at Berry. I didn't know.

"Newkirk. On Jack's Mountain."

"Damn," he repeated. "What do you say in a case like this? 'Oh, good, it's some other poor slob?' "

"It's a girl, they think."

Kirby shook his head. "Well, I'd better get back. Oh, hey. Have you seen Rick Whitman?"

"Jenny's brother? Last time I saw him it was at the garage, in the summer sometime."

"He owes me money."

Berry chuckled. "In that case we won't tell him."

"You seen him?" Kirby rounded on her.

"I was kidding! No, I haven't seen him."

He nodded and rolled the window up. I heard music turn up through the glass and returned his wave as he pulled slowly away. For a long moment I watched the truck, then looked back at Berry.

"He's strange," she said.

"Why do you say that?"

"He's worried about hubcaps?"

"You wouldn't understand. It's a male thing."

"Oh, puh-lease! Are we going to run some more?"

"Are you nuts?"

She laughed and shoved away from the fence with a groan. "Maybe you're right, Jeff," she said, holding her sides. "Oh, brother, are we in sad shape, or what?"

"Speak for yourself."

We walked back to the car, feeling the chill of the weather and the trembling in our legs.

"Want to come home and have supper with us?" I offered.

"Yeah." She grinned. "That'd be nice."

The way her wet hair lay on her cheeks made her look fragile somehow. I liked it.

We sat in my room, rubbing our heads with towels. Berry was wearing one of my T-shirts over her damp sweatpants.

I was tired—relaxed between shivers—and figured I'd probably eat like a horse and sleep all night. I had needed to get rid of a lot of tension. The run had been a good idea. But for some reason I couldn't tell Berry.

"I wonder why Jenny's brother owes Kirby money," she said out of the blue.

"You still think Kirby's selling drugs?"

"You don't, obviously."

"He could have done some work for Rick. That's how he gets *some* money."

"You said you didn't know if he got paid."

"I said I didn't know if his *father* paid him. Dad's given him a few bucks for help with his car and so have plenty of other people." I draped the towel over my shoulders and reached for a comb.

"I'm just thinking out loud here, okay?"

"Think away, pretend I'm not here."

"Hard to do, but I'll try," she said. "I don't know Rick Whitman, but then, if he was buying drugs and planning to skip the payment, why would he pick Kirby, his sister's boyfriend?"

"Can we stop now?" I asked. "Right now I don't care why anybody owes Kirby money."

"You told me to go ahead and think." She sniffed the air. "Mmmm. Something smells good. I think I'll go ask if your mom needs any help." She left the room, taking the wet towels with her. As soon as she'd gone, Katy came in.

"Hey, Jeff?"

"Yeah?"

"Is Berry staying for supper?"

"Yes."

She propped a knee on the bed. "I like Berry," she said.

"Well, Berry is sort of like family."

"Do you still like Amy?"

Katy was the first one to ask the question, but I'd been waiting for someone to do it. After all, Amy and I had been going out for several months.

"Yes, I still like her. We haven't gone out in a while, that's all."

"Why not?"

I threw the comb on the dresser. "I don't know, Katy."

"Do you like Berry?"

I fought back impatience. "Yes, Katy. Berry's a good friend. To all of us."

She nodded. "Mom said that sometimes only an old friend will do."

"She did, huh?" It seemed that Berry and I had become a topic of conversation in the house. It annoyed me.

"Yeah. She said that since Mike . . ." She hesitated at the door. "I'm glad that wasn't Mike they found."

I could only nod. Alone, I stared into the mirror.

Supper was sort of fun. Dad laughed at Berry's bad jokes, and Katy, who had always envied Deena for having a big sister, sat elbow to elbow with Berry, copying her moves: a bite of meat loaf—a bite of meat loaf.

Later, after I'd taken Berry home, something tickled in the back of my mind. I remembered that I'd forgotten something. I bit down hard on my lip, trying to call it up, but nothing came. Approaching it another way, I ran through a list of people in my head.

Kirby caused another tickle. It had something to do with Kirby.

Chapter 8

It seems like whenever you hear a word you've never heard before, you hear it at least twice within days. It's funny how stuff works like that.

The day after Berry and I ran in the rain I was feeling the fuzzy onslaught of a head cold. Everywhere I went I heard talk about the body, which was to be expected. Everyone assumed it was Staci Hartman, who'd disappeared one day after classes at Eisenhower, our rival high school. When added to the Mike mystery, it made for a pretty dark day.

But what got my attention was the number of times I heard Rick Whitman's name.

Now, Rick was older than any of us. He'd graduated two years before. Rick was as notorious as you got in a small town. He'd enlisted in the army and was out within a year, carrying an honorable discharge and driving a new car. Since then he'd worked at odd jobs and hung around whichever group of tough guys was hot at the time.

Apparently Kirby had spread the word that he was looking for Rick, but it seemed that no one had seen him for a while. I still couldn't get rid of the feeling that I was forgetting something where Kirby was concerned, and the Rick Whitman saga kept the tickle going.

I ate lunch by myself. Berry had Molly and someone else with her. She waved to me and sneezed.

I watched Kirby eat his lunch. He seemed out of sorts, chewing viciously and keeping pretty quiet while his buddies carried on as usual. Was Rick bugging him that much? Maybe he was bugged a little by my staring at him, but in any case he shuffled his way over and sat down across the table from me.

"Whatcha doin'?"

"Nothing."

He nodded, sighed, sucked on his teeth. "You hear anything on the body?"

"No more than you. Just rumors, maybes." I was used to this, too. People seem to think I have an inside track on police matters; they don't know the pig story. "No one's seen Rick, I take it?" I asked, watching his face closely.

"No. I'm screwed, that's all." He looked down at the table, leaned an elbow on it.

He wanted to say something else, I could see it on his

face, so I kept silent. He opened his mouth a couple of times, only to sigh. Finally, I cleared my throat.

"Kirby, man, what's wrong?"

"Huh?" He looked up, eyes wide. "Huh? Somethin' wrong?"

"With you. What's wrong? Trouble with Jenny?" That was innocuous enough.

"Jenny!" he said with a huff. "What a flighty snit. Smart as a bag of skunk pelts, that girl."

"Why did you go back with her, then?" The idea of Kirby trying to find an intellectual equal almost made me laugh. "Since when do you want brains in a girl?"

He screwed his mouth up and shook his head. "I thought you were quicker than that, Jeff."

"Well, I guess I've missed something here," I said, and began to stuff trash into my lunch bag.

"I'm putting up with Jenny for one reason only. Wherever Rick's holed up at, Jenny will stumble over him eventually. I've just got to wait."

All of a sudden a chill ran down my back. I was glad not to be Rick. "Just how much does he owe you?"

Kirby sat forward and lowered his voice. I found myself leaning toward him. "I think he owes a lot, to a lot of people, not just me. I'd be doing us all a favor."

I laughed nervously and shook my head. "If you knew what that sounds like . . ."

The bell rang. He left me sitting there, staring after

him with what was probably a really stupid look on my face. What was this? Kirby talking about doing someone in? I'd known Kirby for a long time. I'd seen him lose his temper, threaten fights, and get into a few. But I'd also seen him hold a newborn kitten like it was made of soap bubbles. I'd never seen him like this.

It must be Mike, I thought. Hadn't Kirby said it was freaking everybody? Anyone close to Mike found their brains not working right, their nerves on end. I'd probably read more into Kirby's words than he'd meant.

At dinner I had a headache and left the table without eating much. I took a dose of nighttime cold medicine and went to bed at nine.

Sometime during the night I came awake enough to hear the thoughts pouring past my brain. Jagged snatches of everyday life. They went by me like a train, with no time to reach out, grab one, examine it.

Amy, with a pout: "You look so darn sad, Jeff."

"That doesn't mean you can't dream about a dog wearing a bow tie every night for a week."

"The pig story nearly always applies, Jeff."

"You gonna take over for him now, is that it? You gonna light candles and pray to statues for me?"

Theresa, clutching her scapular. "I thought I saw something at the barn."

Kirby in his truck, writing down mileage. "The damn player in here eats tapes."

Berry and me running on the track in the rain, seeing Kirby. Berry gasping, "You been listening to the radio, Kirby?"

I forced myself to sit up, threw my legs over the side of the bed. There it was, the tickle. The thing that had been bugging me was Kirby's tape player. He'd said it ate tapes, yet that day at the track he'd been using it. Evidently he'd gotten it fixed. So what? I felt stupid.

I also felt hungry. I headed into the kitchen and made myself a plate and heated it up. I had just started eating when Dad walked in.

"I smell food," he said.

"What are you doing up?"

He pulled a beer from the fridge. "Heard somebody out here. Mind if I sit?"

"Go ahead." He didn't ask, but I told him, "I woke up hungry. I didn't eat much. This cold isn't helping either."

"Your Mom said you were out in the rain."

"Berry and I went running."

"You've been seeing her quite a bit."

"Some," I said. I ate, knowing he was watching me. I wondered what ran through Dad's mind when he was in bed, between waking and sleep. We were so quiet it made me jump when he spoke.

"I'm worried about all this, Jeff. About you."

I shrugged. "There's nothing we can do."

"You feel chained down, don't you? You feel like

there's something you ought to be doing, but you don't know what it is."

"That's exactly how I feel."

He nodded. "Sometimes, when I've gone down every avenue six times and come up empty, I have to remind myself that all I can do is sit and think. And wait."

"Is that where the police are? Thinking and waiting?" I heard Mike telling me I had to do the thinking because his head hurt.

Dad cocked his head to the side. " 'Fraid so." He looked at me. "It's not like giving up. It's just that there is only so much . . ."

"I know, Dad."

"Good. Yeah, good."

"The investigators talked to you, right?"

"Yes."

"They know he's an okay guy who wouldn't just . . ." I wanted to say that he wouldn't just run away, but I couldn't. If he had gone off on his own it meant he was okay.

"They know what type of kid he is. All parents say their kid couldn't have run away, but it's not the truth most of the time. In Mike's case they heard it from everybody they talked to, including myself, including you."

I'd always remember being questioned about the last time I saw Mike. How Dad and I sat here at the kitchen table, talking to one of the investigators. Dad had shown the man out, then had a private chat with him that I didn't hear.

In Dad's eyes I saw the things he wouldn't say. Maybe some of them were things he couldn't make himself say, the way I couldn't say them. Hadn't Dad spent time with Mike since we were little? Hadn't he taken me and Mike on camping trips and fishing?

I wouldn't—couldn't—ask Dad about Staci Hartman. If it turned out to be her, how would her parents deal with it? They'd been hoping she had run off on her own, and I knew how much easier that would be to accept.

I finished my late supper and Dad finished his beer, and together we set the table to rights. He snapped off the light as we left and squeezed the back of my neck with his big hand as we parted.

I found Mike at the lockers, where I always found him.

"We're at the end of the line, Jeff." He smiled when he said it. "Things aren't going on like this forever, you know."

"You okay?" I looked hard to see any sign of blood, on his hands or on his head, but the light was in my eyes, putting him in the dark. I could see half his face, and a leaf in his hair.

He ignored my question and hit the locker with his fist. "You aren't paying attention to the obvious, man. I know it's not your fault, but you gotta pay attention to the obvious!" *Rap, rap, rap,* he hit the locker.

"I'll try."

"You know it already, you found it, you just don't realize. You have to think, put it together."

"I will, honest to God I will."

"Nobody came to help," he said, shaking his head. "Kirby . . . I kind of thought Kirby would help."

"Mike, don't give up!" My knees were giving way, crumbling under the guilt I suddenly felt. I put a hand out to steady myself; it brushed against his as it pressed against the locker. He drew back.

"It's okay, Jeff," he whispered as he backed away. "It's just not fair, that's all." He clapped a hand to his chest. "Not fair. I want to come home."

That gesture: He'd done it before. "What did you lose, Mike? Tell me."

"It doesn't matter. Watch yourself, watch Kirby."

I couldn't move to follow him as he disappeared. I stood there, my hand on the locker, until I was alone. The tilting floor and the light righted themselves. As I went to pull my hand away I looked up at it.

Right above it, the locker's tag said NO. 1121.

"Today's the twenty-first," Berry said, her eyes wide. "Today's eleven twenty-one."

"I know that," I said. "Is that what he meant about the obvious? I don't know. This one was so different—"

I stopped when Berry's hand gripped my thigh.

"You know what?"

Just as I was self-consciously edging away from her hand, she slapped my leg hard. "Ow! What?"

"I don't think it's the date! Come on." She got up and slung her purse over her shoulder.

"Berry—"

"Come on!"

I grabbed my books to follow her.

"What's this about?" I asked in the hall.

"Mike's always at the same section of lockers, right?"

"Yeah, but . . . You think it's really the locker?"

"It's no crazier than anything else, Jeff. He said you never notice the obvious."

I looked around hopelessly. "But everything looks different in the dreams."

"Then let's look for the number. We have twenty minutes to find it before lunch lets out. Then we—"

"We what?" I interrupted. "Stake it out?"

"So are you coming with me or not?"

We found it outside the shop room. Number 1121. Chills ran up my back as I looked at it, and I tested myself by putting my hand on it just like I had in the dream. It didn't bite.

"You okay?" Berry leaned against its neighbor.

"Yes."

"You look sort of white around the gills."

I threw her what I thought was a devastating look. "Sometimes having a cold will do that to you."

"That again!" She pushed away from the locker. "Man! I didn't *force* you to run."

"I'm sorry," I said. I was taking things out on her.

I dared another look at the locker tag. It didn't cause any reaction this time, and I felt better.

"We might not even know the person who has this locker, if he or she shows up," I told her.

"There's a good chance they will."

People usually went to their lockers after lunch. And if they weren't on the same lunch we were on, they would be on the next.

We moved over to the water fountain when the bell rang. I had no desire to get in the way of whoever it was. And as crazy as Berry's idea sounded, I wanted it to be the answer. I wanted to see someone come down the hall, stop and open the locker, then turn around so I could see their face and have the answer fall in my lap.

"Jeff," Berry whispered.

I saw him. He opened No. 1121 and threw a book into it before pulling one from the top shelf. Like in the dreams, the hall felt as if it was tipping down toward the bank of lockers, and I leaned back against the tiled wall. When he shut the locker and turned, he saw us.

I waved and pulled Berry with me as I headed in the opposite direction. But not before I saw Kirby wave back.

Chapter 9

I went half nuts the next few days. I kept my distance from Kirby, afraid to talk to him about anything in case I got that weird feeling and said something I'd regret. An uneasiness had taken hold of me, and I couldn't shake it. I felt like I was hanging on to a runaway jackhammer.

The dreams were definitely real. I knew that the moment I found locker number 1121 and saw Kirby open it. If the locker was real, then the blood on Mike's hand was real, and worst of all, his warnings were real.

What did Mike mean when he said, "Watch yourself, watch Kirby"? Why did he stand in front of Kirby's locker? Why did he tell me to get Kirby in those other dreams?

These questions kept going through my mind along with others they generated. What had I already found? Why was I supposed to watch Kirby? What was I to watch for? I thought of Kirby's words about Rick Whitman. Was I supposed to stop him from whatever he was planning to do to Rick? Or was he in danger from Rick? It all made me so damn dizzy, dragging me one way, then slamming me against the opposite wall. The night before Thanksgiving I found myself begging Mike to come in another dream. But he didn't.

On Thanksgiving morning I awoke to the certainty that Mike was dead. I knew it like I knew my name. And I knew it was just a matter of time before somebody found him. *"We're at the end of the line, Jeff."*

The noise of company—cousins and grandparents, aunts and uncles—filling our suddenly small house made a dent in my sullen mood. I found I could talk without my voice breaking, and even laugh. Mike's name wasn't mentioned, not in my presence anyway. I was hungry, ready to eat anything that even hesitated for a moment on my plate.

I guess it was because I was feeling so good that my sanity returned and I started to feel bad. Not a bad bad, but a good bad. I thought of Berry and how I'd cold-shouldered her after finding the locker, as if it was her fault.

Later I grabbed the phone and went to my room. I sat down on the bed and dialed Berry's number. Deena answered.

"Deena, hi. Let me talk to your sister."

"Oh, hiya, Jeff!" It seemed a long time before Berry

got on the line. She sounded put out, but quietly so. You know, like someone would if they thought you were crawling for forgiveness and they wanted to make it worth your while.

"Jeff? You want me for something?"

Ouch. "Uh, not really." Damn. "Well, actually . . ."

"Jeff?"

"No. I don't want anything from you. I wanted to talk, that's all. Okay? Can we talk?"

"About what?"

"Darn it, Berry! I don't know . . . just anything! I'm sane today, at least I think I am. I know I've been acting weird and I'm sorry, okay?"

"Jeff, it's okay. We never talk about anything but the whole dream mess and I don't seem to be helping."

I took a deep breath and lay back to stare up at my ceiling. "Okay. How was your dinner? Did you have company?"

"Huh!" she said. "My cousins Demon Seed and Spawn of Satan are here now, throwing pool balls around the basement. They're too rowdy for Deena, even."

I laughed. "Ah, the four-year-old twins."

I half listened as she talked about her family and the holiday job she wanted to get at the dime store. I couldn't help drifting from it, wishing I could let go of things the way she seemed able to do. So it caught me off guard when she stopped.

"Jeff? I'm sorry, but I need to talk to you about it."

"What's bugging you?"

"It's the dreams." She sounded apologetic. "There's something I don't think you're aware of. You know you can't always look at it from a distance like I can."

"You're the one who said it's all we talk about."

"I know, and I'm sorry. Can you call me tomorrow sometime? I can't talk now. It's so noisy here, and I have to think, make it plain."

"I'd rather see you. Name a time and I'll pick you up."

"How about anytime after lunch?"

"That's workable," I said.

"Okay."

"So," I said. "We're done pretending we can avoid the subject."

"I know," she said. "We have to deal with this. See it to the end, whatever that is."

"You've been like a padded room for me, Berry," I told her. "And I mean that in the nicest way."

"You don't need a padded room, Jeff. All you need is answers."

"Do you have them?"

"No. But I don't think I have to tell you who does."

We went to the track and sat in the windswept top row of the bleachers. We had a nice view of the deserted parking lot.

"When's your first track meet?" Berry asked.

"April. Come on, Berry. Talk."

"The way I see it, Kirby is the key. I don't know any other reason for Mike to bring him up all the time."

It kind of spooked me the way she talked about Mike. She repeated Mike's words as easily as she would Deena's, or mine, as if there was no difference in the way they were first said.

"I still have trouble with the whole dream-message concept, Berry."

"Yeah, well, concepts suck, you know? Look, you have to ignore the concept and take the experience for what it is. That goes for most things, paranormal or not. Talk about concepts, how do you like the concept of light-years?"

"What?" I gaped at her.

"I'm serious. In one second a beam of light travels seven times around the earth, can you believe it? That's like three hundred thousand kilometers. The sun is eight light-*minutes* away, but it's not a measure of time, it's a measure of distance. That's eight times sixty seconds at three hundred thousand kilometers each. Now—"

"Wait, wait!" I held a hand up to silence her and rubbed my eyes. "This is confusing and I don't see how it—"

"I know it's confusing to us, but not to an astronomer who relies on light-years to pinpoint positions of stars. I have no problem with the way Mike has been telling you things, because I think differently than you do. I know it's possible."

"You're saying that I don't have to understand the way Mike comes to me in the dreams. Right?"

"Right."

"So, he's telling me things about Kirby. You think Kirby knows more than he says."

"That's just it, Jeff. What has he said?"

I shrugged and squinted up at the sun, light-minutes away. "Berry, he doesn't know anything about Mike or he would have said so."

"Do you know that for sure?"

"Yes." No, I thought. How could I? "But I want to know why you're so sure he does."

She sniffed and tucked her chin into her coat collar. "Mike said he thought Kirby would help. Why?"

"You tell me."

"Okay," she said with a sigh. "He said you didn't come. Why do you think he expected you to?"

"Because he told me to. You know that." I kicked the bench in front of me and turned to her. She wore a satisfied smile on her face.

It dawned on me slowly. "You think Kirby had a dream too."

"I'd bet the house," she said.

"No way. He would've told me."

"Like you told him about yours?"

Man! "I tried to tell him. I said I had a dream about Mike. He would've said so, right there. Besides, Mike could have meant that Kirby didn't help me."

"But you haven't come right out and asked Kirby to help. So . . ."

"So?" I asked, not liking the look on her face.

"Well, I'm assuming Mike knows what's going on, okay? He seems to know you found whatever it is you've found, right? So if Mike didn't send Kirby a dream, and knows you didn't talk to him about it, there could only be one reason he expected Kirby to help somehow."

"Don't say that." No way. No way that Kirby knew where Mike was. Especially since I was sure Mike was dead.

"Well, I guess it's possible Kirby had a dream *after* yours. Maybe you should talk to him again."

Berry had a point. Maybe if I had laid it all out for Kirby to begin with, I wouldn't be stewing over it.

"There's one other thing that's bugging me, Jeff. There are two ways you can take Mike's warning about watching Kirby."

"Meaning?" I waited, knowing I wouldn't like one of them.

"Well, the way you took it, of course, then . . ." She sighed and looked at the track, not me. "Or he could have meant it like someone would say, 'Watch out!' "

After a long silence her eyes came slowly back to mine.

"You don't like Kirby, do you?"

"Jeff! I don't know him to dislike him. We have to look at every possibility until we know which is the right one."

It only made sense. If sense fitted into this anywhere, we had to insert it ourselves.

"Let's go," I said, and stood up.

Berry nestled in the passenger seat and turned on the radio.

"You want to practice driving?"

"You mean it?" She sat up with a grin. "Sure! Where?"

"Let's go up Shivers Lane and out to the orchards." There were miles of less-traveled roads out that way.

I couldn't help grinning with her. I was suddenly in a good mood, shelving the serious stuff for later. We turned onto Shivers Lane and I began telling her the story about Theresa at the barn. "She says she saw something. I don't know what."

"That's neat. I was always disappointed as a kid, didn't see so much as a cat there."

"You believed the story?"

She laughed a little. "Maybe I wanted to believe it. Didn't you?"

"I guess." I was thinking of how I had gone back to the barn the next day, and the way things hadn't felt right there. I automatically slowed the car as we neared it.

"You know," I said in an offhand way, "I came up to check the place out later. See if there had been anybody up here."

"I take it you didn't find anything."

"Just a bunch of trash."

"We can look again."

"Want to?"

"There's no time like the present," she said even as I was pulling over.

When I turned the car off, I looked at her. "I don't really know why I'm doing this." She was out of the car and climbing the bank before I opened my door.

I didn't even notice the tire tracks in the brown weeds until I topped the foundation and saw the truck. The blue pickup sat parked behind the foundation. Berry was standing by it, running her hand over the hood.

"They haven't been here too long," she said. "The engine's still warm."

I looked around at the woods. "Probably a hunter. Gun rack?"

She looked into the truck and nodded. "Kind of late in the day to start hunting, don't you think?"

"Maybe he just got off work. In any case we shouldn't get too close to the woods." I made my way back over to the foundation and began poking around. "What am I looking for?"

Berry came up beside me. "What do you *think* you're looking for?"

"I have no idea. Theresa saw something—somebody, maybe."

"There's plenty of human stuff here," she said as she kicked a beer can. Her breath froze on the air.

Just around my feet I saw three beer cans, a couple of fast-food wrappers, and a used condom.

"Hey!" Berry yelped. "I found a quarter!"

"Lucky you," I said. Then I got that feeling, the one I'd had at school the day I told Berry I thought Mike was dead. I stood still and glanced over at Berry. Did she feel it too? But she was busy raking her sneaker over the stubbled ground, eyes down.

Someone was watching me, us. Looking over my shoulder, I couldn't see anyone.

A hunter would be wearing camouflage, and I might not be able to see him if he was far enough into the cover of trees.

"Come on, Berry. Let's go."

"What?" She looked at me, then at the woods.

"Do you see anybody?" I couldn't make myself look again, and the feeling was as strong as ever.

"No." Her eyes came back to mine. "But maybe we should go." Without waiting for me, she went to the edge and jumped off the foundation. I followed her without looking back.

Chapter 10

After we left the barn Berry drove for an hour, taking curves with care and letting go on the straights, which dived and climbed the hills full of gnarled trees. "Be a hell of a time to get a flat," she said once as we sped downhill. I laughed but found myself gripping the door handle.

At home, I took a long shower and let the hot water relax me. I put on boxers and a T-shirt and opened the bathroom door to find Dad leaning against the opposite wall.

"Jeff." He pushed away from the wall and put his hand on my shoulder, steering me toward my room. "Something . . ."

"What is it?" I settled onto the edge of my bed, watching him shut the door. "Dad?"

"I think we've found Mike, son."

There it was. It was suddenly, horribly, the end of the line.

He took a deep breath. I looked away from his face, let my eyes go down his body. There, at the hem of his tan pants, was a rim of stain. His shoes had been wiped but shined through muddy smears. "Oh, God. Are you sure?"

"Officially, no. But I know . . . I knew Mike. We're getting the dental records."

"Where?" I was swallowing back nausea. My head buzzed as I stared at those muddy shoes.

"Shivers Lane. Behind the barn."

"No." I shook my head, felt my jaws clench hard.

"Two hunters, in the woods."

"The blue truck," I said, and stood up, going for the dresser.

"What?" Dad moved aside as I pulled open the drawers, pulling out socks, jeans.

I flung the clothes on the bed. "Berry and I were just up there after lunch! We saw the truck, knew someone was hunting!"

"What, today? You were up there today?" His hand grasped my shoulder.

I stopped, looked at him. He'd seen him. He'd seen Mike in God knew what condition. Suddenly I recalled a time ages ago when he came home late, stripping his clothes off as he walked to the shower. He said he wanted to get "it" out of his nose, off his skin. It wasn't

until much later that I'd realized he was talkin
the smell of a body.

"Berry was practicing her driving . . ."

He rubbed a hand over his face. "Jeff, I'll tell yc
I told his parents."

The Thayers! My heart flipped over once anc
Theresa's face, freckled and smiling. "What?"

"I . . ." He cursed under his breath and movec
door, wrapped his hand around the knob. "I didn
him. I watched every step. I closed the tailgate
wagon."

"Dad—" I'd only seen Dad cry twice in my lif

"And I promised him, Jeff. I promised him."

"No, wait!" I said, and grabbed his arm as he
the knob. "You have to tell me, Dad. He was . .
head was hurt, wasn't it?"

Dad's eyes widened the slightest bit, his
opened. "Jeff, I want to know why you asked me

It wasn't interrogative; he sounded afraid. I let
him and felt my face go hot. "You wouldn't believe
don't believe it myself." I sank down on the bed
put my head in my hands.

"You wouldn't lie to me. I know that."

"It was a dream, that's all. I knew he was dead f
dream, and his head . . ."

Dad bent over me and wrapped his arms aroun
"I'm sorry, Jeff. Are you going to be okay?"

I nodded. "I'm going out," I said. "Something I have to do."

"I don't think you should go anywhere right now."

"Dad, I'm not asking permission." I stopped to get the shaking out of my voice. "I have to get out of here, just for a while, you know? Just for a while."

"All right." He let me go. "But I'm here for you. You come talk to me anytime, Jeff."

The door shut and I was still sitting there when I heard the hum of water running in the master bathroom.

My headlights bounced on the wall as I pulled into Kirby's parking lot. He was at the desk in the service station and looked up as the brakes squealed. Leaving the car running, I opened the door and jumped out. He met me in the doorway.

"Whoa there," he said, stopping me with a hand on my chest.

"Mike's dead, you know that?" I was screaming; I hadn't wanted to scream at him. "Hunters found him in the woods, you know that?"

His hand dropped away and his face went slack. "Mike?"

"He was waiting for us, man! He was waiting for *us*!"

"Stop it!" He slapped at my jabbing finger and gripped me by the arms, shaking me like I was a ten-year-old.

"Behind the barn!" I shouted through rattling teeth. His forearms were solid beneath my hands.

"*Jeff!*" It came out in a roar, stopping me cold. My hands eased up and the shaking ceased. "For Christ's sake, what are you saying? They found Mike?"

"Yes."

When he let go of me I almost fell. I followed him into the station and sank down in the chair by the gumball machine. The odors of diesel and oil drifted around me. It smelled hot. Service stations always smell hot.

"Jesus Christ." He put his head down on the desk. I shifted in the seat, licked my lips.

"I want to know what you know about it, Kirby." Blood pounded in my temples as I waited.

The kerchiefed head rose, the blue eyes met mine with ice. "I don't know crap."

My heart hammered. "I think you do."

"Says who?" He leaned back, the swivel chair groaning under him.

"Mike."

"Mike. You just said Mike's dead."

"He told me that—"

"Who told you what?" he interrupted angrily.

"Mike! I had dreams—"

"Oh! Good!" He laughed and grabbed the bandanna from his blond head. "Jeff's having dreams now."

"I told you I was having dreams a long time ago. The night you were working in the garage! And again at the diner."

"That's right, you did." He let his head fall back and he turned the chair to the right, took out a cigarette, and lit it. Black-rimmed nails waved as he shook out the match. "So, what did Mike tell you in these dreams?"

"I can't really . . ." How was I going to figure out why Mike expected Kirby to come to him too? "It wasn't in so many words, Kirby, but I think you know something."

"Like I said, I don't know crap. And those dreams may slap you in a loony bin if you go around telling people about them."

"I haven't told anybody but you."

"Well, thanks." He stood up and went to the door. "Look, I'm going to close."

"Go ahead, close. We'll talk."

He grabbed me by the arm. "No. You're going to leave."

I flattened myself against the door, spreading my arms wide. "Kirby, I'm going to find out what happened to Mike. You can help me."

"No! You're going to keep your nose out of it! And if that girlfriend of yours is helping you, you make sure she does the same." He pulled me toward him so he could open the door, then let go. "Bye."

"Kirby—" I tried once more.

His eyes shut and he bit down on his lip. "For Christ's sake," he said quietly, "would you leave now?"

— — —

I pulled up in front of Berry's house. What was I doing here? I was about to restart the car when I saw her dark shape come from behind the house. She beckoned me back there.

Shivering in my jacket, I headed for the backyard, hands in my pockets. An image of Kirby's face moved a step ahead of me, frustrated, tired, sad. But always angry.

"Berry?"

"Here." She was on the dark patio, standing behind a telescope. "I was almost expecting you, Jeff."

"You know." Her voice had told me.

"Come here." She moved aside and I bent my head to look through the eyepiece. A cloudy splotch met my gaze.

"Nice," I said, and sat down on the wooden bench behind her. "I saw Kirby. Told him I had a feeling he knew something."

"Jeff!" She spun around from the telescope. "Not now! You shouldn't have done that *now*!" Her breath smoked in the cold.

"Now. Before. What difference does it make?"

"What did he say?"

"Said he doesn't know crap."

Berry sniffed and brushed a gloved finger under her nose. She pulled a tissue from her pocket and wiped her eyes.

Berry had cried. Dad had cried. Even Kirby had looked like he was about to cry. What the hell was the matter with me? Mike was my best friend, and now he was dead.

She bent to the eyepiece and I went to stand beside her.

"What is that you're looking at?"

She straightened, sniffed. "It's the nebula in Orion."

"Orion. The hunter, right?" I felt it then, the stab behind the eyes.

"Yeah." Softly.

"We were there when they . . ."

"I know."

I stepped off the flagstone patio onto the wet, cold lawn. I couldn't hear her but knew she was there, just a few paces behind me. At the end of the yard, by the row of bare rosebushes, something caught up with me. The strength went out of my legs and I knelt down in the dead grass.

"Don't sit on the cold ground, Jeff," she said.

All I could think of was Mike sleeping on the cold ground for all those nights, waiting for me to come find him. He'd been there when I took the kids to the barn; he'd been there when Berry and I walked in the foundation. It was him who had been watching me from the woods, thinking I had come at last.

The tears ran hot down my cheeks and I went forward

onto the icy lawn. I could taste the earth in my mouth, and I heard Berry's quiet sobbing as she got down beside me. Her upper body and arms covered mine. And as her hair fell near my cheek I realized I'd picked the safest place to cry.

Chapter 11

The next night I sat in the den with Dad. We had gone there to talk, but so far, nothing had been said. I studied the circles under his eyes.

"Will I need to give another statement, Dad?"

"I don't know. Probably not. You last saw him at school, not afterwards. He left his house at six-thirty." He sat on the coffee table across from me. "Tell me about the dream you mentioned." He loosened his uniform tie and cleared his throat.

"Wait. How did he die, do they know?"

He hesitated, but I sat still, staring him in the eye. "The coroner's preliminary said it was a gunshot to the head."

My stomach lurched and I gripped the arms of the chair to keep myself in it. "Yeah. He wiped his hand over his head like this," I said, showing him, "and it had blood on it." Dad paled and I felt the words forcing themselves up my throat. "I knew he was in the woods too. Not any particular woods, but woods, because he had leaves in his hair and he was muddy, and . . ."

"Slow down, Jeff," he said, reaching forward to pat my hand.

I took a deep breath and told him about the dreams. I left out Kirby's name because Berry had me so paranoid about Kirby and whatever involvement he might have. I emphasized Mike's appearance and the way he said he had lost something.

"But, Dad, I let him down, because he was waiting, you see? He expected me to come find him, and I didn't."

"Jeff, listen to me. They were dreams, okay? Now, I can't explain the blood and the leaves, but I know there is no way in hell Mike would have wanted . . . that."

I slumped, put my head back and looked at the ceiling. "I guess it was pretty bad, finding him."

"Don't think about that. We've found him, and now we can work on finding whoever did this to him. If you hear anything—"

"I know. No matter how unimportant it may seem."

"That's right." Dad's big hand slapped mine again and he got up, headed for the doorway.

"Dad, you said you promised Mike something."

He stopped, turned. "I did. I promised him justice."

I stood up and moved to his side. "After all this dream stuff, I believe he heard you."

Dad squared his shoulders and looked me in the eye. "I meant him to, Jeff."

"Maybe you should tell him about Theresa seeing something at the barn."

Holding the phone, I rolled over onto my back and kicked my shoes off. "I can't do that, Berry. Not now, after he already thinks I'm wacko because of the dreams. Besides, we don't know what she saw."

"You believed her enough to go look. Suppose there *was* somebody there? I know it was weeks after Mike's disappearance, but it's not impossible for it to have been somebody who knew about him."

"Yeah, yeah, the classic return to the scene—"

"Do you know if it actually was the scene? Did you hear something?"

"Well, no." I'd never thought about it. It could have been just a place they picked to dispose of him. A chill ran down my arms at the thought. You dispose of trash, not a person. I worked the spread out from beneath me and slipped under it. "Have you heard anything that suggests it wasn't?"

"No. But you know we *wouldn't* hear anything."

I decided this was a good place to bring up Kirby to her. "Last night when I saw Kirby I asked him if he'd help me find out who killed Mike. He threw me out, told me to stay out of it."

"What? You didn't tell . . . He said that?" She sounded frightened.

"Berry, I'm sure—"

"This was after you asked him what he knew about Mike's death? Doesn't that strike you as strange, Jeff?"

"No—I don't know."

"Did you tell your dad?"

I hesitated. I wouldn't tell Dad anything that was mere conjecture, even if he did want chapter and verse. "Berry, I don't want to sic the cops on Kirby. I don't think he's guilty of anything, I swear. He and Mike—"

"He and Mike had arguments about *praying*, Jeff. Who knows what else they argued about? If Kirby cared so much for Mike, why doesn't he want to help you find out who did it? It sounds more like he's throwing threats around."

"I'm not convinced, Berry. I don't know why. I need something more than what we've got, which, *come on*, is nothing! If I see something, hear something—"

"You heard a threat," she said coldly. After a pause she sighed. "What can we do, then? What do we need to do?"

I rolled to my side, smiling into the phone. "All we can do right now is keep our ears open, maybe watch Kirby a little—"

"You said—"

"Berry, I said I'm not convinced. It doesn't mean I can't be convinced." An idea struck me. "Hey, you know how he kept turning up at the diner and the track?"

"Yeah. He said he saw your car and stopped."

"What if we were to pop in on him instead?"

"Huh?"

"Look," I said. "Do me a favor. Do you think you could call McDonald's and get Jenny's schedule for this week?"

"I know a guy who works there. . . . It's worth a try."

"I don't think Kirby's given up on finding Rick yet. He's probably still going to get her from work, taking her out, and trying to pump her brain, which he swears she doesn't have. Maybe we can tail them, bust in on their chats." Once out, the idea sounded lame.

But Berry said, "That's good! We'll be able to tell a lot just by the way he acts around us, don't you think? He's probably too smart to let something slip, though."

"You think Kirby's smart?"

She laughed.

A comfortable silence went by. Then Berry cleared her throat. "Have you heard anything about a funeral service yet?"

"I don't know if they've released his body yet. When I know something I'll tell you."

"Good, because . . ."

"You'll go with me, Berry, okay?"
"Of course."

Three days later she stood beside me at the grave site. A lot of kids who had taken the day of amnesty from school had been to the church for the funeral mass, but the number of them had dropped at the cemetery. I hadn't seen Kirby at either place.

My father and I acted as pallbearers, at Mr. Thayer's request. It was the hardest thing I've ever done. I'll never forget the way my father looked at me, his eyes full, and I knew he was thinking, *How do you bury a son?*

It was sunny; the tree line spiked along the pale sky. Mike was being interred in a spot not far from the large plot of Civil War dead; the flag in the middle of their ground snapped in the breeze. I watched the priest, only partly listening to the blessings he was saying over Mike's casket.

Center front, he waved a silver censer over the flower-strewn mahogany. His robes were a stark white point of focus in the darkly clothed gathering. My mother had whispered that the Catholic priest wore white as a celebratory color because Catholics believe there is rejoicing when a soul goes to the Lord. How she knew this I didn't ask.

Then, as if on cue, the Thayers began to move forward. I watched as Mike's parents knelt and kissed the casket, took a rose from its lid. Theresa was moving forward; then she stopped and turned. Her eyes found mine and she started toward me. I took a couple of steps to meet her and bent so that she could whisper in my ear.

"Jeff, you come with me," she said, taking my hand.

I looked back at Mom. Her face had crumpled into tears. "Okay, Theresa." Holding her hand, I walked to the casket, saw Mrs. Thayer smile, and knelt with Theresa.

She slowly pulled a rose from the spray and handed it to me. Her freckled cheeks were wet and my heart turned over. I put an arm around her and held her to me.

"I wish I could make this go away for you, Theresa."

She tucked her face into my neck, then pulled away and leaned toward the casket.

"Mike," she whispered. "Jeff will be our big brother now, don't worry." She selected a rose for herself. I saw her take something from her coat pocket. "Here," she said, setting it down on the casket, "it's like your old one."

As I stood with her, my head buzzed. I looked down at the jumble of dark ribbon she'd set on the flowers, which joined two pictures of the Virgin attached to small squares of brown cloth. This was a scapular like Theresa's white one, and I realized it was worn with one plastic-coated square hanging in front and one in back. But there was *something*, a memory pulling at me.

I rejoined my family and felt my mother's hand slip

into mine, but couldn't grip it in return. I handed the rose to Katy, who had cried to me that morning, reminding me that Mike had asked her to marry him when she grew up. I waited for the service to be through, the people finished with choosing their flowers and saying good-bye.

Finally I was able to go to Mrs. Thayer. She hugged me. I didn't know how to broach the question in any other way but to come out with it.

"Mrs. Thayer, Theresa gave Mike a scapular."

"Yes." She crushed a tissue in her hands. Mr. Thayer stood a few paces behind her, protectively.

"Didn't Mike wear one? A brown one?" I felt my face go hot with my guess.

"Yes, he did. All my children do, as a symbol of faith. Old-fashioned or not."

"But she said it was like his old one. Wasn't he wearing it?"

Mrs. Thayer wiped her eyes again and pulled me closer. "I was told not to say anything, but I don't see why I can't tell you, Jeff." A chill raced down my back as she looked around. "Mike wore his scapular pinned inside his T-shirts. When they found him . . ."

"It was gone?"

"Yes!" she whispered, and tears ran down her face again. "Everything, the scapular, the pin . . ."

I stood there as she turned back to her husband. I

stared at the casket as others crossed in front of me, leaving the grave site. Dad put a hand on my shoulder but I shrugged it off.

"I'm staying awhile, Dad. I have to make sure of something."

Dad, clearly misunderstanding, said, "It will be a while before they lower it, Jeff."

I swung around to face him. "No, I . . ."

"If you don't feel up to stopping by the Thayers' I'll excuse you."

"Thanks."

Then it was just Berry and me by the coffin, being watched by the guys who pulled up in their truck and waited to bury Mike. I knelt down and touched the scapular, pushed it around with my fingers. I laid my hand over the pictures and looked at the dark ribbon that curled amid the leftover flowers. I'd seen it before.

It was like driving along and having a rabbit or a cat jump out in front of your car. In one timeless moment your heart leaps into your throat as your foot goes to the brake. That's how I felt when I remembered where I'd seen it. I jumped up.

"Jeff, are you all right?"

"Berry." I turned and took her shoulders in suddenly icy hands.

"What is it?" She looked as scared as I felt.

"God, Berry. I . . . Come on," I said, and started

toward my car. "Did you get the schedule, Jenny's schedule?"

"Yes. Tell me—"

"We've got to make some plans to accidentally run into Kirby. And I've got to get into his truck."

Chapter 12

A chance to get into Kirby's truck. That was the only thing that made me decide to go to school the day after we buried my best friend. Mom was surprised and insisted I take the car in case I wanted to leave.

At school there was a large notice on the office door saying that crisis counselors were available for any student who wished to talk about Mike's death. On my way to homeroom several people stopped me to say they were sorry, or to tell me about the assembly they'd held for Mike the day before the funeral. I felt myself nodding and trying to smile, but couldn't help thinking they were waiting for me to fall apart.

My mind wasn't on any of my morning classes. I kept running things through my head over and over. New class, new run-through. I hadn't seen Kirby's truck when I parked, but I was going to check for it again at lunch. If it was there, I'd see if it was unlocked.

I knew what Mike had lost. I could see him again, slapping his chest. He'd lost a scapular that I hadn't known he'd worn. It was brown. If you'd never seen one before, the ribbon of it could look like a cassette tape come unwound, especially if only partly seen in a messy glove compartment.

It was an unbelievable picture, Kirby killing Mike and for some reason taking the scapular from him. If Kirby had killed Mike, what was his reason? If he didn't have something to hide, why did he tell me to stay out of it? What was he afraid I'd find out? The whole thing gave me a headache.

By the time I got to the cafeteria I knew Kirby wasn't in school. I usually passed him in the halls twice before lunch and, not having seen him, I'd scanned the parking lot before joining Berry.

"Where can I find out about scapulars and stuff?" I asked.

"Ask his mom, I guess." She waved to Molly, who was in line with a tray. "Is Kirby here?"

"No. And I can't ask Mrs. Thayer about scapulars now, she's got too much on her."

"You could go to the church, then. Ask a priest." She slapped the table. "Oh! Jenny gets off at ten tonight."

"Can I pick you up at nine?"

"Fine. Remind me to tell you what I saw today," she said as Molly made her way to the table.

I sat there for a few minutes while Berry and Molly made chitchat, then got up to go. Berry looked at me.

"Nine," I said. I felt her eyes on my back until I was out of sight.

The secretary at the rectory said Father Chris was around somewhere and to make myself at home. I sat in an overstuffed wing chair in the cozy room. The table beside me held a copy of today's newspaper. For the first time in days Mike's name was not on the top half of the front page.

Suddenly I thought of Amy. In English class she'd handed me a plain white envelope.

"I know you probably have this, but . . ."

"What is it?" I took the envelope and began to open it. She stopped me.

"It's the obituary, Jeff. From the paper."

I watched her cheeks flush pink. "Amy?"

"I just didn't get to say how sorry I am," she said, and blinked back tears. "I couldn't throw this away . . . you know."

"Thank you."

"If you want to talk or anything, call me."

Amy faded from my thoughts when Father Chris entered. He wore a red sweatsuit and sneakers. I rose to shake his hand. "What can I do for you?" he asked, then sat down across from me.

"I'm Jeff Owens, Father. I can come back if this isn't a good time."

"Oh, no. I just came in from a run. So, Jeff, how can I help you?"

I told him I was Mike's friend. He seemed to settle then, leaning his elbows on his knees, and I noticed the way his smile lines left ghosts on his face when he wasn't smiling. He wasn't as young as I'd first thought. He listened as I brought up the scapular.

"I don't know why, but it seems like . . . Well, he wore it all the time, and so it must be more than . . . I mean, I know it's not a charm or anything. But I'd like to know what it is so I can . . ."

"You want to understand why he wore it, is that it?"

"Yes," I said, relieved he didn't look at me like I was asking a stupid question.

"There are different scapulars."

"Mike's was brown."

Father Chris sat back and crossed his arms over his chest. "The Scapular of Mt. Carmel. It's said that the Virgin gave that scapular to St. Simon Stock in the twelfth century as a sign that the Carmelite Order . . ."

Now it was the priest who was stumbling on words. He cleared his throat.

"That's not what you want to know, though, is it? That isn't why Mike would wear it. People wear them for different reasons. Some wear them as a daily reminder of their faith, and perhaps others because of the promise the Virgin made to the saint when she gave it to him."

"Promise?"

"It used to be taught that those who wear the scapular faithfully and fulfill the other obligations are assured they will be delivered from purgatory after death." He cleared his throat again.

"What exactly is purgatory?"

"It's a place that is neither heaven nor hell."

"Who goes to this purgatory?"

"Some would tell you just about everyone."

The room felt suddenly hot. "It doesn't sound like a good place."

"It separates one from God until one is free from imperfections." He leaned forward again. "I'm afraid this isn't helping you. It's too involved to explain in a few sentences, though."

I could hear Mike, what he said in the dream. *"I'm nowhere, man."*

"Father, if Mike wore the scapular but it was taken from him and it wasn't his fault, he'd still be protected, right?"

"I don't think Mike wore his scapular because of any promise, Jeff. I found Mike's faith to be unusually strong, trusting, and assured for a boy his age. As I told his mother—I'm assuming she told you about his scapular—if I answered that with my heart, I would say that I know Mike is with God right now."

"His mom, yes." I hadn't even thought about it. Besides his family, this priest, and the police, I might be the only person who knew about the scapular—except for the killer.

I studied the priest's face. His brown eyes practically begged me to believe him. I should have felt immediate relief.

But Father Chris hadn't had a dream.

Berry and I parked at the far side of the McDonald's lot where we could see the front doors.

"I guess they're not going to tie Mike's death with Staci's," Berry said.

"They haven't said yet. There are as many differences as there are similarities, I guess." I had a feeling the police would never tie them together, even though it would put some kind of reason to Mike's death. Small-town serial killer who went after regular, good-kid teens. Great.

"Anyway, Berry, I was supposed to remind you to tell me what you saw today."

"Oh yeah. This morning, on the bus, we were almost to school and I saw Jenny talking to Rick."

"You sure?"

"I know it was Jenny," Berry said. "She was leaning on the fender and talking to Rick through the window. So, what do you think, Jeff?"

"And are you sure it was Rick?"

"Yes. It was his black Pontiac, anyway."

"It looks like Rick's not hiding out after all. Not if he's going to meet his sister out in the open."

"Maybe he's not afraid of Kirby," Berry said. "Maybe it's the other way around."

"I don't get it."

"What if Kirby wants to get Rick, not for money, but because Rick knows something?"

I couldn't get the picture of a scapular in Kirby's glove box out of my head. But even if it was a scapular, did it really mean Kirby was involved with Mike's death?

"Let's wait and see what I find in the truck, then we'll figure out the other."

Berry shifted in the seat. "If you find it, what are you going to do about it?"

"I'm not sure."

"We have to tell the police."

She was right again, of course, but I didn't answer. I looked at my watch for the hundredth time.

"I'm going to run in for something," Berry said.

"What if he comes while you're in there?"

"He won't think we're here to spy on him, anyway."

There was no sign of Kirby while I waited for Berry to return. She came back with two cups of cocoa.

"Suppose he doesn't come for her tonight?" I took the lid off my cup and blew across the surface. The smell of chocolate wafted up into my face.

"He will. She waited on me and asked if I'd seen him outside."

The cocoa was so hot I couldn't taste it. I blew on it some more. Berry began trying to cool hers too.

"Then we wait," I said.

A minute went by and it was starting to sound pretty wild in the car, what with all of the huffing and blowing on our cups. The windows were fogging up. Berry started laughing first, a slow giggle.

"I was trying to ignore it." I laughed with her. She looked so cute there, holding her steaming cup away from her and hiding her wide grin with her other hand. I moved her hand away and leaned toward her.

"Jeff," she said, just before someone knocked hard on my window. I jumped and hot cocoa sloshed over my fingers.

"Da— Ouch!" I handed the cup to Berry, and with my wounded hand I rolled the window down. "Kirby. What's up?"

He smiled lazily and dipped his head down to look into the car. "Nothing that fun," he said. He shoved his hands into his pockets.

"I looked for you at lunch today," I said.

"You did, huh?"

My insides were jumping, but except for Kirby's normally threatening posture, he didn't seem edgy. I gave Berry a sidelong look and got out of the car. I needed to get some kind of reaction from him.

"I wanted to apologize for the way I broke the news to you that night. Never in a million years would I have wanted someone to do that to me."

"Don't think about it," he said as if I'd only stepped on his toe. "You were freaked, that's all. After you left, I freaked out awhile too."

Hard as I tried, I couldn't tell if he was lying or not. "Well, I just wanted you to know I was sorry."

Kirby flung a big hand out to clap me on the shoulder. "Catch you later, Jeff." He walked off toward the restaurant.

I opened the door and sat on the edge of the seat.

"Where's his truck?" Berry asked.

"I didn't see him come in. I might only have a minute. Here, give me the cups."

I took the cups and set them down on the pavement. "Slide over here and follow me with the car, but stay where you can see them coming."

I took off in a sprint around the back of the building. His truck sat alongside the Dumpster. Looking back, I saw that Berry was now parked at the corner, where she could warn me.

My heart raced as I tried the passenger-side door. It was locked, and I ran to the driver's side. It opened, the light pinning me to the seat. If Berry yelled, I'd never hear her over the blood rushing in my ears.

I scrambled up and reached for the glove compartment. For one instant, while my finger rested on the release button, I hesitated. Then the image of Mike slapping his chest gave me courage. It opened, bounced on its hinges. Reaching inside, I played spread fingers over the contents. Nothing that felt like a ribbon.

"Aw, come on!" Bending down to look, I saw that it wasn't there. Just as I shut the glove compartment and jumped out of the truck, Berry pulled the car forward.

"Shoot!" I slammed the door shut and stepped up to my car, waving Berry to her seat. She threw the car into park and slid over as Kirby and Jenny came into sight.

"Kirby!" What was I going to do now?

"What are you doing, Jeff?" He looked at me, then at his truck. I wished I'd just made a run for it.

I pulled my wallet out. "You didn't get to the funeral, so I thought you'd like one of the cards." I'd grabbed several cards from the funeral parlor. I hadn't known they could cover my butt.

Kirby reached out and took the small card. It had a picture of Christ on the cross, with a prayer for Mike on the back, under his name and the date of his disappearance. Kirby's cold blue eyes met mine and he blinked. "I just didn't feel comfortable going, you know?"

"I'm cold," Jenny whined from the passenger side.

"Get in, then," Kirby snapped, pushing the card into his pocket.

"The door is locked!"

"For Christ's sake. Gotta go, Jeff."

I got into my car without another word, my hands trembling as I shut the door and pulled away.

"It wasn't there," I told Berry.

"Did you get a good look, though? You didn't have much time. It could have been—"

"It wasn't there, Berry."

I didn't know what to think. Had it been a tape after all? Or had he taken it out because I'd seen it? Worst question of all: Had I shut the compartment securely? I got an awful chill picturing Jenny in the seat, saying, "Why's this hanging open?"

As the quiet drew on, I grew calm again, the questions receding for the moment. Maybe now Berry would drop this Kirby idea of hers. Part of me was beginning to wonder if Berry realized I'd almost kissed her.

So it rocked me when she said, "He must know they're looking for it."

Chapter 13

Things were really screwed up. I'd missed two tests in school that had to be made up, let college application papers sit blank on my desk. I couldn't seem to concentrate on anything but Mike and Kirby.

I'd screwed up with Dad, too. He cast worried looks at me over the dinner table and in the den at night. I shouldn't have told him about the dreams and then gone running off to play cops with Berry on these missions he knew nothing about.

Even without the scapular Berry was positive Kirby knew about the murder, one way or another, and I didn't know how long she'd stay quiet. I couldn't give myself one good reason not to tell, except for my years of knowing Kirby. But somehow, I couldn't tell anyone.

It seemed there were two of everyone. Two voices in my head: one against Kirby, one for him. Kirby went from the good-time Kirby I'd always known to a colder, harder Kirby who wouldn't even go to Mike's funeral. Even Mike seemed to have an alternate. I didn't know the Mike that Kirby knew. Kirby had hinted there was a lot I didn't know about Mike.

On Saturday I had an overwhelming urge to go to the Thayers' house. I hadn't seen any of them since the funeral and I often saw Theresa's face when I closed my eyes at night. I'd told her I wished I could make things go away for her, for us all. She seemed to take it as a promise of sorts.

To get the car from Mom I agreed to drop Katy at her gymnastics class.

"You have to walk her in, Jeff, don't just drop her on the curb."

"All right."

"And you have to go in before class ends at one. Watch her tumble a bit."

"I will."

So I drove Katy to the school. She was suited up in a tiger-striped leotard under her winter coat. A yellow puffy band held her hair up in a ponytail. She looked serious.

"You don't look like you're up to this today," I told her.

"I can't keep my right arm straight."

"Oh. Work on it."

She sighed. "I *am* working on it. I can see it in my

head, and I tell my arm to stay straight, but I fall on my shoulder anyway. How come I can see it but not do it?"

"I don't know, Katy, I just don't know."

I arrived at the Thayers' a little after eleven. Frank opened the door and let me in. "Jeff's here!" he yelled. Months before, anyone opening the door to me would simply have called out, "Mike!"

"Come on up," Mrs. Thayer called as Theresa and Marie came out of the kitchen. They ushered me up the stairs to Mike's room. I hesitated at the door.

"Girls, let Jeff and me visit awhile. Did you finish the dishes?"

"Swept, too," Theresa said.

"Thank you. Take the laundry down to the basement now."

"Okay." Theresa flashed me a grin and left.

I stood in the doorway watching Mrs. Thayer pull things from under Mike's bed. Frank and Jimmy had the left side of the large room, their bunks covered neatly with striped spreads. Mike had never complained to me about sharing his room with them.

"Come in, Jeff."

"I didn't know you'd be doing this," I said, grasping for words to fit my feelings. This shouldn't have been done until Mike went into the navy, or off to college.

"It makes me angry, having this stuff here making it

hard on everyone. You know, the police came after he was found. They came in here and tore out all his drawers, tossed his part of the closet, you name it. I know they had to, but it frightened Jimmy, and he slept on the sofa until the room was straightened. Once it was, I thought it had been a waste of time. So I'm clearing out. Frank can take this bed, and Philip can finally get out of the cot."

She stopped and looked at me. "I'm sorry for rambling."

I sat on the bottom bunk, finding it hard to look at Mike's bed. "Is there anything I can do?"

"No. I wouldn't ask you. But if there is something of Mike's that you want, please don't hesitate to ask, Jeff."

I shook my head. "His brothers should have his things."

She straightened and set a box labeled WINTER on the bed. "I can hardly believe it, but sometimes I think it's good that we had a chance to get used to being without Mike before they knew he was dead. Can you understand that?"

"Yes." She seemed about to cry, and I stood up. "I thought I'd spend some time with the kids before I have to pick Katy up at gymnastics. Do you think they'd like it?"

"They'd love it. I've kept them busy all morning. Jeff, I know what Theresa told you at the funeral about being their big brother now. Don't worry yourself or feel obligated. It was just her way of telling Mike they were taken care of."

"I know how she meant it, but it's something I'd like to do anyway. Mike would like me to take over for him."

She smiled. "He probably would."

"So it's okay if I hang around awhile?"

"Oh, Jeff. Don't ever ask me that."

The five kids were rounded up and we walked out back to the swings. Frank said he was too old to swing and Jimmy climbed up into the bare oak. Mike had hammered wooden pegs into the trunk, up to the vee, two summers ago. Theresa, Marie, and the youngest boy, Philip, each took a swing.

"Sounds like you guys are being good and helping your mom," I said as I pushed Marie. Frank was pushing Philip, and Theresa had already gained a lot of height on her own.

From the tree Jimmy said, "We're always good."

I laughed to myself. "That's great."

"Have you been good, Jeff?" Marie asked.

"Pretty good, I guess."

"Jeff's always good too," Theresa said. She let her head fall back and grinned at me upside down as she went feet first into the winter sky.

Frank stepped back from Philip's swing. "How long do you think it would take to fix the Chevy? Dad says it would be years before I could drive it, anyway."

The question made me happy all of a sudden. "Really? You want to take over the work now?"

"Yeah, I was thinking about it."

At nine, he had a good seven years. "It will be a classic by the time you drive it. You'll be a real hotshot."

"That's what I figured. I just have to learn cars."

"Don't look so smug, Frank. Learning cars, as you put it, can take a while."

"I know. But Jerry said he'd help me."

"Jerry who?"

"Jerry Kirby. Who'd you think I meant?"

Marie's swing bumped my leg. "When did you see him?"

"Last night," said Jimmy from the tree.

"He came by and talked to Dad about the car," Frank said. "He had some cool hubcaps he said Mike wanted."

"That was nice of him."

"Yeah, and he said he'd bring me some book that Mike had borrowed a couple of times too."

"Jerry didn't let us pay for them either," Jimmy added.

"Do you want to see them, Jeff?"

"Sure, Frank. Let's go."

We left the others at the swings and Frank slid open the heavy wooden door on the old garage. The Chevy's bulk loomed in the dark shed. How many times had I sat there, on the dirt, while Mike tinkered? We stirred up the dust and I could almost hear it swirling around me until Frank spoke.

"Right, here they are."

He handed me one of the shiny chrome hubcaps. "It looks brand-new, doesn't it?" I asked.

"Only one of them has some rust pits in it and Jerry said he'd keep an eye out for another. They're from a seventy-eight."

My reflection stared up at me from the chrome.

"You okay, Jeff?"

I saw the same look in his eyes. "Sometimes I am. Sometimes I'm not."

He took the hubcap from me and nodded. "Me too," he said.

"Watch me, Jeff."

Katy stepped up to the mat and squatted down. She did a perfect somersault.

"That was great," I said. "What are you complaining about?"

"Now watch." When she rolled backward her right arm gave way and she fell over onto her side. She jumped up. "Why does it do that?"

I went to the mat and squatted down. I somersaulted backward with no problem. "I don't know, Katy. Let's see what you're doing wrong." We worked on it until she had managed one perfect backward roll. By that time we were so dizzy we staggered out to the car, laughing.

I was making sure Katy's seat belt was tight enough when I noticed the pickup. I shut her door and walked around the front of the car to open mine, watching Kirby idling up the block. I waved. Kirby did a U-turn and gunned away. He didn't wave back.

On our way home I couldn't help being distracted by all Mike's Missing Person flyers that we passed. If they distracted me, how much more did they bother the Thayers? I called Berry and she agreed to help me pull down what we could that night so the Thayers wouldn't see them on their way to church in the morning.

At nine-thirty I was waiting for her at the diner. An hour before, I'd dropped her off at the south side of town and I'd taken the north. Town's not so big. We have two—count 'em—two stoplights, on the main road, each a block from the square.

I was drinking a soda when Berry came in. Her cheeks were colored with cold and I smelled the night air that shook from her coat when she took it off. She smiled as she slid into the seat across from me. She ordered cocoa. Chin in hand, she looked at me. "So did you get your area covered?"

"Yeah. You?"

"Clear."

We sat in silence until her cup arrived.

"Mom thinks we're dating," she said, watching the waitress walk away. "I didn't know what I should say."

"My family is thinking the same, but I haven't said anything to them."

"So, let's decide," she said.

"Okay. Let's let them think it."

"Just pretend?" She looked down at her hands.

"For now." I felt rotten saying it. Spending time with Berry had been what I needed to do in the beginning. Now, I realized, I wanted to see her. But I couldn't act on it yet, not with everything like it was.

A silence settled between us. Was she feeling as awkward as I was? To get past the moment I said, "Play a game with me, Berry. It's called Good Kirby, Bad Kirby. Which side do you want?"

"Gee, take a wild guess."

"Okay, I say the good side and you rebut with the bad."

She smiled, lazy-like. "Shoot."

We leaned over the table toward each other and looked around.

"Okay. I know your interpretation of 'Watch Kirby,' so I won't even ask that one. But how about when Mike told me to get Kirby? I think he wanted me to bring Kirby in on the search."

"Maybe," she said in a low voice to match mine. "But he could have meant he wanted you to 'get him' literally. Like 'nab him.' "

"Kirby was scared at the track when we told him about the body being found, and relieved to find out it wasn't Mike."

"He could have been scared," she said. "But I'd be scared too if I killed somebody and didn't want him found. As far as relieved goes, I don't call asking us about Rick Whitman relief."

I drummed my fingers on the tabletop, searching for my next call. "That day he also mentioned the hubcaps. I just found out he took them to the Thayers' house and offered to help Frank with the car."

"Maybe he wants to get in good with the family. What better protection?"

"You're pretty good at this game, Berry."

"You gave me the easy side. Let me go first now. The scapular in the glove compartment."

"Ah, but it wasn't there later, and now I'm not even positive it was a scapular I saw."

"Fine, I'll forfeit that one. How about how he threatened you after you told him you wanted to find out what happened to Mike?"

"You ought to be a lawyer, Berry."

"Can't you give me a good side to this?"

"He could have said to stay out of it in order to protect me."

"Which in my book," she said, leaning closer, "smells like knowledge. How do you warn someone of something if you know nothing about it?"

"You can't jump on my rebuttal like that."

"Who says?"

"Me. It's my game and now it's over." I reached for my glass but Berry stopped my hand with hers.

"Jeff, don't be angry. I think it's a good game. It made

me see the other side. Now I know why you have doubts."

I slid my hand out from beneath hers. "I could say the same to you."

"Wasn't that the point of the game?"

"I didn't realize the good side would be a harder sell."

Berry combed her fingers through her curls. "Look, even if Kirby's the right guy we still don't have a motive. Without motive there's no case."

"I'm surprised you don't have one all worked out. From the start you've been after a Kirby connection."

She sat back and crossed her arms defensively. "You wanted to play cops. Cops look for motives."

"Do you or don't you have a theory?"

"Not starting with Kirby, no. We have to start with Mike. Most murders are the erasure of a threat, don't you think? What kind of threat did Mike pose to someone?"

I thought about that. I watched the traffic and the front of the Majestic Theater, vacant while the last showing was in progress.

"It's useless," I said finally. "Everything's been said, we know what's there. . . . It's got to be something we don't know, or else it would be kicking us in the face."

"Or something we know but haven't considered."

"Mike said it was all there, to put it together."

"But we can't just jam it together." Her hands compressed the air between them and locked fingers around it.

"He prayed for Kirby," I said, noting her hands.

She placed her palms flat on the table. "You pray for someone who is sick or in trouble. Was Kirby in trouble?"

"Or headed for it?"

She nodded. "But not just any trouble."

"Illegal stuff."

"Probably. I'd say drugs." She stirred her cocoa and smiled a little. "But you knew I'd say that."

"Before I could, anyway."

Her eyes grew soft. "This isn't fun for me, Jeff. I don't like to sit here and make you turn one of your friends into an ogre who could have killed another friend."

"You aren't making me do anything."

"I'm glad you feel that way. I only wish I could make you talk to your dad."

"Don't start—"

"Jeff, please."

"—that again."

Berry held both hands out, palms facing me. "Fine." She drank her cocoa and stared daggers out the window.

I wanted to ask her, *What keeps you from telling your dad?* But I was afraid it would sound too much like a go-ahead.

Chapter 14

It was snowing lightly.

At least, that's what the guy on the radio was saying when the alarm went off in my still-dark room. It was Sunday and I didn't have to get up, but the night before, after the not-so-friendly parting with Berry, I'd decided to go back to Mike's church today.

The idea had come to me as I'd driven by the church on my way home, when I remembered that Mike had told me he'd served as altar boy for the early service. I decided to go, even though it was at six o'clock. I don't know what I was hoping for. But Mike would have been going this morning if he'd been here.

I left a note for my mom on the table and stepped outside. It *was* snowing. Sparkling polka dots floated through the light on the post at the edge of the driveway. Half of me shivered and asked the rest of me what the heck it was doing. I chose Dad's car, knowing I'd be back before he was up, and the windshield cleared easily with a brush of my sleeve.

Me and the early-morning Catholics, I thought. We owned the morning when soft snow falls and the hair in your nose crinkles with each breath. But that thought left me soon enough, when I started driving toward town and passed bread trucks and dairy trucks. The almost romantic feeling stayed with me, though, and I got the notion that I was getting a peek at an elite club made up of morning people.

I was a bit surprised to see the number of cars parked along the curbs near the church. Going up the steps and through the heavy doors was easy. But as I faced the long aisle to the altar, where candles were being lit by an altar boy, I was struck with doubt.

I didn't belong here. And even if Mike had been alive and lighting those candles himself, I wouldn't have been here to see him do it. I didn't want to think about it, though.

There were about twenty people in the pews closest to the altar. I followed a man partway up the aisle, then stopped. I watched him continue to the front, kneel briefly, then kneel again at his seat. My left knee bent to the floor beside a pew without my telling it to, and I edged in to sit down.

I chased the doubts from my mind and decided to just experience the moment. The wavering light from the banks of prayer candles made shadows dapple the carved face of the Virgin Mary, who stood in a niche on the left. On the right, her counterpart, a bearded man with a staff, looked down, with heavily browed eyes, at his own bank of candles. Between them, behind the altar, was a life-size painting of Christ, hand raised in blessing. Father Chris entered from the right, hands clasped at his chest.

It was strange and wonderful to me. I watched the mass in silence, not bothering to follow the moves and words. Most of the people attending were elderly, their voices soft and their words unhurried as they responded to the priest's. They rose and sat and knelt as one.

Father Chris seemed to notice me just as I was wondering how he could say the same words countless times and do it with such sincerity. His eyes moved over the people before him, then lifted to include me. I felt his greeting.

I'd only seen the sacrament of communion once. It had been at Mike's funeral but, sitting with my family, I hadn't taken special note of it. Now I watched as Father Chris raised the bread and wine in turn, said the words that held the others rapt. There was something in this mysterious rite that I could not catch hold of, but I could feel it.

When the people began to move forward to receive the wafers, I had to fidget in my seat to stay put.

I knew they believed the wafers had been transformed into the body of Christ when the priest prayed over them. I'd gathered that from the prayers. Maybe it was the mystery, or maybe it was because I had no firm belief in anything, but somehow, watching these people take the wafers into their mouths, I almost believed.

Then, suddenly, I remembered a nighttime swimming party Mike and I had gone to, and how we'd left it in full swing.

"I've got to be at church before six in the morning," he'd said. "You can come back, but drop me home, will ya?"

"Sure. But why get up that early on a Sunday?"

He shrugged. "I'm used to it. A lot of old people go early, they've been doing it all their lives. I look at them and see all this strength. Each one of them has a whole lifetime of faith behind them."

I hadn't understood at the time.

Now I sat waiting for the service to come to its end, wrapped in a quiet peace. There was no ongoing argument in my head, no ache in my jaw. I felt a crazy hope that things would get better for me, that one day the turmoil would be gone for good.

Father Chris gave the final blessing and left the altar, and the people filed out. Several of the ladies looked curiously at me as they passed; one smiled broadly, her round cheeks pushing her eyes closed. Still I sat. The altar boy put out the candles and ran past me moments later, zipping his coat.

I was still there when Father Chris came back to the

altar again, this time in an overcoat. He prayed beside the altar, then stepped down onto the main floor.

I thought he would ask me what I was doing there, and wasn't sure how I'd answer him. I looked him in the eye when he stopped beside me.

"Jeff, isn't it?"

"That's right, Father."

"How are you?"

"Okay, I guess."

He smiled. "I must admit, you gave me quite a start this morning. This is typically a senior citizen do, you know."

I laughed with him. "I'm glad I came, anyway."

"I'm glad you did too. You're welcome anytime." He offered his hand and, as I shook it, he said, "Stay as long as you like. Soak up the quiet."

He was nearing the doors when I called him. He stopped.

"Mike told me he liked the early service."

Father Chris scratched his chin. "I could always count on him. Personally, I always thought it was because the ladies gushed over his curly hair." He grinned. Then he nodded. "I'm glad to know he liked it as well."

I felt my gut tighten. I hadn't thought that he might really know Mike, that he might be feeling the loss too. He seemed to be waiting for me to let him go.

"Thank you, Father."

"Anytime, Jeff."

I was alone. When I heard the outer doors shut, I turned and studied the altar until a little of the peace I'd felt during mass came back to me. In the silent church I opened my mouth.

"Mike."

It seemed to vibrate in the wavering shadows on Mary's face.

"Mike, I didn't come when you needed me to, and I'm sorry."

I waited. He owed it to me to answer my apology. But nothing came and I could feel the muscles in my jaw begin to tense again. I spun around in the aisle and ran from the church.

That Sunday turned out to be the Great Welcome to Winter Cookout. My father had started the tradition several years back, when my mother was cleaning out the freezer and wanted to use up a pack of steaks.

Dad had called some of his friends to join us, and as he stood outside grilling the steaks in the cold, almost everyone had ended up out there with him. After dinner we'd played a game of tackle in the snowy yard. Those who couldn't come for the day had stopped by for a quick meal. It was such a success that we held it every year, and this was the first time since then that we'd had snow to go with it.

Though the games of tackle grew shorter each year, a new tradition had seeped in. There would be six or seven guys climbing around the house later, putting up Christmas lights.

I was in a pretty good mood. It was fun to watch my normally fastidious mom bundled up in a sweatsuit, rushing around with rosy cheeks. She wasn't pulling the door shut tight behind everyone as she usually did, or biting on her lip until we wiped our feet properly.

Out back, under a hastily erected lean-to, Dad was grilling chicken, fish, burgers, and whatever else had been brought.

Berry and I were sitting at the front window, watching for cops. When a patrol car pulled up, we'd go to the kitchen and fix a plate of food for the new guests, who would go out back to visit with Dad.

Berry was in a good mood too. She hadn't brought up our Good Kirby, Bad Kirby game. It was like nothing had happened. She sipped hot cider and joked and laughed, swinging her long curls over one shoulder or the other.

I could have sat there forever, but I heard music, and knowing it was my stereo, I jumped up. "Be right back."

Katy and Deena were on my bed, singing.

"You could ask first, Katy. I don't want you fooling with this."

She sat up. "Deena can work it. Do you think I'll get a CD player for Christmas? I asked Mom for one, and she said to ask Santa. Deena has one."

"A kid one," Deena said.

"We'll see what Santa brings," I said.

"Guess I can wait a couple of weeks."

A couple of weeks. I looked at the calendar. With a jolt I realized I hadn't turned the months over since September. Everything had seemed to stop for me on one September afternoon. My head buzzed a little, like it had when Dad told me they'd found Mike. I reached for the calendar and ripped it from the wall, flinging it to the floor.

"Jeff?"

Katy was staring at me. Before I could say anything she was out the door, Deena on her heels. I started after them, then stopped, turned, and paced back to the spot where the calendar lay, open to September. The day he disappeared, the day they printed on the cards as his disappearance date, glared up at me. My foot ground down on it.

"Damn you, Mike!" I yelled with the music. Raising my foot, I stomped on it over and over. *Nowhere, man. Nowhere.* "You should've thought of that before, man! But no. You had to pray about it to some statue instead of telling me what was wrong! Had to keep it to yourself, whatever it was. It's your fault if you're nowhere, because it's all your fault that somebody put a goddamned bullet in your goddamned head!"

I picked the calendar up and hurled it. It struck the mirror, pages rattling. I stared at myself, my reflection giving me the same look I'd seen on Katy's face.

You look crazy, the reflection said.

Chapter 15

I was facedown on the bed when Mom came into the room. I knew it was her; Katy would have run to tell her, not anyone else, that I was in the bedroom cracking up.

"Will you be coming out?"

I didn't answer. I was feeling ashamed and a bit scared of the way I'd gone weird.

The bed sank under her weight and her hand began patting my back. "I don't know what to say to you, Jeff, but it's okay. You haven't made time for yourself to digest what's happened."

I rolled onto my back. Her rosy face was serene, as if she didn't have three other things going already in the kitchen, as if she had all the time in the world to sit at my side, just waiting for me to open up to her. But that was something I couldn't do right now, because opening up would be telling her everything. What would she say if I opened my mouth and said Kirby might know something about Mike?

She would probably think back on what she knew about Kirby. She'd always been polite to him, had never said anything to me outright. But a guy knows what his mom is thinking just by the look in her eye. He can tell the difference when she looks at someone like Kirby compared to the way she looks at someone like Mike.

"Are you going to be okay?"

"Maybe one day."

She thumped me on the chest and smiled. "I knew it was an unanswerable question the second it popped out."

"I'll be out in a minute or two. Tell Katy I'm not crazy or anything."

"She knows that."

After she left, I went to the bathroom and washed my face with cold water. Coming out, I ran into Berry in the hall.

"You checking up on me too?"

She pushed past me, a wounded look on her face. "I have to pee, if that's okay."

Great. I thought about the peace I'd had at Mike's church that morning and wondered if I'd ever get it back. I put my coat on and joined Dad at the grill outside. The snow was soft, and each step packed it down to a glossy shine.

"Hey there," Dad said.

I had come outside mainly to escape the house, and now I didn't want to be here, either. There were two off-duty friends of Dad's out here, one of them John Murphy, Berry's dad; and there was one on-duty trooper in full uniform, his hip radio talking away. Melted snow beaded on his shiny black shoes.

You'd think I'd be used to it, but there was still something a little awesome to me about a uniformed trooper. The tan slacks with the black stripe down the outside of the leg, the black leather jacket with its patches and heavy silver snaps, and the hats with their patent brims, shining like the shoes. Add the radio. Then the holster.

How many times had I seen my father run the creases of his uniform pants through pinched fingers? Hundreds. How many times had I seen him polish shoes, or insignia, or tie clasp? Thousands. How many times had I seen him clean his gun? Never. I'd only ever seen Dad's gun holstered, just as I was seeing this trooper's weapon.

I glanced at Dad, who was talking with John Murphy and cooking chicken. I looked back at the gun. Dad had always warned us about the danger of firearms and had taught us to stay far away from them. His gun was cleaned at the station or outside the house, and we weren't allowed near it. At home it was locked in a box he kept hidden.

I remember Katy asking to see it once. Of course she

didn't get the privilege, just as I hadn't at six years old when friends thought it was cool to have a cop for a dad. Dad had said, "I hope to God you always fear guns and what they can do to you."

"Are you afraid of them?" Katy had asked.

"I respect them. I never let myself forget what that gun can do."

"Jeff?"

I blinked and turned to Dad. "What?"

Dad and Mr. Murphy laughed. "Didn't you hear me?" Dad asked. "John and I were asking about you and Berry."

"What about us?"

"We just think it's strange that you two have been seeing so much of each other, yet you haven't said anything."

I could tell by looking at them that they weren't asking for serious reasons. They were goading me. "Maybe it's because we were afraid something like this would happen."

They laughed, and I smirked, and all of us felt like we'd accomplished something. Dad covered a bowl with a towel and handed it to me.

"Would you run this in? And ask Mom if she has anything else to go on."

"Sure." The hip radio crackled, and I was heading for the door when I heard the dispatcher say, "Shivers Lane." I stopped. Everybody near the grill stood still.

The on-duty trooper pulled the radio from his waist and held it up in the air.

". . . passerby on a cell phone is reporting several children running around near the crime scene."

"I'll head up there," the on-duty guy said. He handed his plate to Dad and ran around the side of the house. The car started and pulled out before Dad said anything.

"There's nothing up there," Berry's dad said.

"Still, they shouldn't be there," Dad said, shaking his head.

"Kids have always gotten a thrill out of the place," the other off-duty guy said. "Now it's got a little added spookiness."

Then Dad looked at me. "Take that in before it gets cold."

I put a smile on my face before breezing into the kitchen. "Send out anything else that needs to go on, Mom," I said. Berry was standing near the counter and I glanced at her as I passed her on my way to the front door.

I sat down on the front steps. So now Mike's death added spookiness to the haunted barn.

Were the kids just curious? Were they daring each other to find the spot where Mike had lain? Were they looking for something the police might have left behind? Maybe they weren't even aware of Mike. Like the other cop had said, kids were always running around up there.

I heard a car at the stop sign on the corner. A moment

passed and I didn't hear it move. It idled with a low rumble. Finally I looked.

It was Kirby's truck. He moved forward, crossed the intersection, and went past me, gunning the engine and gearing up. He never looked at me.

Just like outside Katy's school the day before, I thought, and I immediately wondered what I'd done to him to make him act this way. A coldness shot through me, and it wasn't from the weather.

By the time most everyone else had left, Berry and I noticed that our parents were casting glances our way as if waiting for us to make an announcement or something. I nipped it in the bud by asking, "Mind if we leave together? I'll get Berry home."

Everybody smiled. Everybody nodded. Everybody ushered us to the door like we were being sent off on an epic journey.

"Cripes," Berry said as we went to the car.

"They like it that we're together."

"But we're not, are we?"

I didn't answer. Instead I said, "I'm sorry I snapped at you today."

"It's okay."

I opened the door for her. "I'll take you home and then I want to look for Kirby."

"No, let me go with you. Just tell me what it's about."

It began to snow again. Tiny flakes landed on her dark

curls and melted. She sighed and her breath misted across the car door to me, bringing me a whiff of cinnamon gum.

"Get in and I'll explain."

I told her about seeing Kirby go by the house. "He wanted me to see him, but he wouldn't look at me."

"That's creepy, Jeff."

I shrugged and started the car. It had given me a weird feeling when he'd driven past, looking straight ahead. It was like he would have sat there idling at the stop sign forever if I hadn't looked up. He'd wanted me to see him the day before, too. When I saw him and waved, he'd left. It was like he wanted to scare me.

"Where are we heading?"

"This is the way Kirby went."

"I don't think you should do this, Jeff. He's acting way too creepy. Why don't you wait to see him at school tomorrow?"

"I could take you home."

"No. I'll go. But you've got to tell me exactly what you expect to happen here."

"Damn it, Berry! I don't know what I'm expecting. I'm just sick and tired of all the stuff that runs around my head day and night. I'm sick of seeing Kirby trying to tell me things that he can't say. And I don't like the way he's acting."

"But what can you do?"

"I'm going to do what I should have done in the

beginning. I'm going to tell him about my dreams and ask him to tell me the truth about anything he knows."

"So now you agree he knows something?"

I rubbed my face in frustration. "I hate this, Berry. I can't make you understand what's inside my head and I'm not going to try."

"I have no idea what you want me to say, but . . ."

"But?"

She turned in her seat and leaned toward me. "I understand more than you give me credit for. I can imagine what kind of mess your brain gets into when you think about Kirby. You're going: 'Did he? Didn't he? Do I give him a chance or do I tell the police?' But you think you can go around hitting Kirby with questions, and that's not smart."

"What can he do to me, Berry?"

"Chances are Mike thought that way too. Did you ever think of that? You have this one picture of Kirby as a murderer and another of him as someone who is going to let you jab at him over and over. The pictures don't mesh, Jeff."

"I never said I thought he murdered Mike."

"Then why all this craziness? You must have thought it at least once or twice. How about at the cemetery when you realized what you saw in his glove box? Why did you check it out if you weren't thinking it?"

I braked and pulled the car over, throwing it into park. "Will you stop this?" I yelled.

Berry groaned and pounded her fists on her legs. "God, Jeff! You just don't get it! Do you remember telling me I was like a padded room to you? Well, padded rooms are there for people who are thrashing around trying to get themselves hurt. I won't stand around with my mouth shut while you get yourself hurt!"

She was yelling and crying, and I felt the fight in me slipping away.

"I'm not going to get hurt," I said quietly.

She sniffed and wiped her eyes. "You don't know that."

"Look here—"

"No, Jeff. You look here for once. I'm not a padded room. I'm a person. And I want you to think very hard about how I'd feel if something happened to you and I thought I could have stopped it."

She grabbed my hand. I felt like a traitor. What would I have given to stop whatever killed Mike?

"I'll be okay. I promise. I'm just going to talk to him."

She sighed. "Then I want you in my sight."

A tear ran down her cheek and caught on her upper lip. There was only one way I could think of to reassure her. One thing I wanted to do. No matter what else was going on.

There was no one coming to knock on the window

this time. I bent my head toward hers and kissed her gently, then kissed the tear away. We looked at each other, and I pulled her wet face to my shoulder and held her, rested my cheek against her damp curls. It wasn't easy to let go.

Chapter 16

I tried the garage first. Mr. Kirby was sitting in the office with his feet on the desk. There were no lights on at Kirby's house. I drove around to McDonald's. The red pickup was parked in the back.

"I'm almost sorry we found him," Berry said.

"Look. You're going to sit here, okay?"

I parked near the edge of the lot, where she would be able to see both his truck and the side of the restaurant. She looked around, then touched my arm.

"Okay. Be careful."

I walked into the restaurant and zeroed in on Kirby. He sat with his back to me. I hesitated for a second, then spun his chair around to face me.

"We've got to talk. Now."

"Whoa, what the hell's the matter with you?"

"I was going to ask you that."

Kirby stood up. "Outside."

I waited for him to put his coat on, and I gestured for him to go first. I followed him as he walked to the back of the lot, to his truck, just as I'd figured he would. If he was going to have to clobber me, it wouldn't be out front for everyone to see. I tried not to think too far ahead, and now that my chance was right in front of me, I didn't know if I'd be able to make sense when I opened my mouth.

"What's your problem?" he asked as he leaned against the hood of the truck.

I watched him light a cigarette. "You're the one with the problem, Kirby. Why are you acting like this, man? Why are you always lurking around?"

Kirby eyed the ground. "I don't know what you're talking about."

"You don't? You just happen to be there long enough for me to look up? You've got me now, right here, so tell me what it's about."

"There's nothing to say, Jeff," he said, his eyes coming up to meet mine.

"I've known you a long time, Kirby, and I know something's not right. There's something on your mind, so talk."

He flicked burning ashes into the wind. "I'm still looking for Rick." A lazy smile crossed his face, like he thought he was conning me.

"Well, he's not at my sister's gym class and he's not at my house."

He snorted and tried to move past me, but I grabbed his arm. "Hold on, Kirby."

He threw the cigarette down and ground it out with a boot heel, then shoved his hands in his pockets and rocked back and forth. His shadow moved with him on the snow-speckled asphalt.

"I don't have anything to say to you, Jeff."

"Then maybe I should do the talking. I came to you once, to try to tell you about a dream I had. Mike told me to get you and come get him. I knew he was dead—"

Kirby's hands came out and shoved me back a step. "I don't want to hear this." I followed him to the side of the truck; then he came at me, pointing his finger and yelling. He backed me up until I was pressed between him and the fender.

"You having dreams again, Jeff? 'Cause maybe you should try sleeping pills or something. Or maybe it's more than dreams, huh? Is Mike jumping out around corners at you, huh?"

I immediately thought back to the night in the diner when Kirby had begun rambling about Mike. Berry had called it dark and depressing.

"No, he isn't." I straightened and he stepped back to let me. "Does he jump out at you, Kirby?"

"Are we done? Because I gotta go in and get Jenny as soon as she's off." He started away from me.

I jumped in front of him, my hands on his chest. He

gripped my wrists and I wondered for the first time if he'd used one of those hands to shoot Mike.

"Get off me, Jeff."

"Talk to me first. Jenny will come out looking for you if you're not there waiting." I just kept blocking him, not knowing if he would punch me.

He was yelling, "Get off. Get away!"

He tried to push my hands away and I grabbed handfuls of flannel in both fists. Then I felt the square of plastic beneath his shirt. My stomach turned. My grip weakened. He brushed me off like a fly.

"You did it, didn't you? You killed Mike."

"You're crazy," he said, and changed course, heading for the truck.

Adrenaline kicked in and I was on his heels, trying to tackle him around the waist. "I didn't want to believe it, but I do now. You took a gun and shot him in the head, didn't you?"

"Get lost, Jeff!" He pushed down on my arms and wriggled out of them, but I jumped again.

"Why'd you do it?"

Kirby swung at me then, and caught the side of my face. I didn't feel it and grabbed his arm, swinging him as wide as I could to get him away from the truck. I wanted to land on him, hold him down, and scream in his face. But he swung again. I ducked and lunged forward, hitting him in the gut with my head.

Then he was on his back and I was kneeling on him,

dodging his fists and struggling to hold on to him. "It was Mike, man! Mike!"

"Get the hell off!"

"You've got his scapular on!"

"He gave it to me!"

We were rolling. I held on to his coat, not wanting him to get completely free. "Tell me the truth, Kirby!" A fist hit me square in the face and reflex brought my hands up. It was all Kirby needed.

He was getting into the truck and I jumped up, grabbing for the door handle.

"*Get out!*" I yelled, and pulled at the door.

My shoulder gave out, the door shut, and the truck started. Kirby looked at me through the window, shaking his head and yelling that I should leave him alone. Screaming inside, I watched him pull out.

"Damn it!" I yelled.

I took a step toward my car. The adrenaline had left me and my legs became nearly useless. I stumbled and landed hard on my knee.

Berry came running up to me. "Jeff! My God, Jeff, are you all right?" She helped me up. "Come on."

"I've got to follow him." I brushed the snow off my knees. One knee was bleeding through a hole ripped in the jeans.

"No, you can't. We've got to wait here."

Then I heard the siren. "Oh, Berry."

"I'm sorry."

"What did you tell them?"

"That you were going to confront him and that we—that I thought he knew about Mike's death. He's hurt you."

"He was trying to get away from me."

I didn't want to sit there waiting while the cops took a statement from Berry. I answered them briefly. "It was my fault, I goaded him," I kept saying. Another cop had taken off in the direction Kirby had gone.

In the end, I refused to press any charges. Berry and I got silently back into the car. I was angry with her, but I could imagine how easily she had found herself at the phone. Besides, I was confused myself. For a while there I had wanted to pound him into the ground, sure he'd killed Mike. But there was something about his face when he told me he'd been given the scapular, something in the way he'd shaken his head.

"Can you drive?"

"Yes, Berry." I was bleeding from the nose, but it was slowing. My top lip hurt and I felt shaky but my head was pretty clear.

When I put the blinker on to turn onto Berry's road she said, "No. I'm going to be there when you tell your father. He'll know something's happened, anyway, and my dad . . ."

Berry was right. I was sure both our fathers had heard what happened. They would probably also know what else Berry had said about Kirby. I felt sick. What would I say to Dad?

Dad came out the kitchen doorway, the phone to his ear.

"I'm glad you're both here. Come on in."

I knew it was the police on the phone. I threw my coat on the couch, struck by the eerie effect cast on the scene by Katy singing Christmas songs in the bathroom down the hall.

Mom spoke first. "Are you hurt badly?"

"Nah."

She pulled a clean dishcloth from a drawer and wet it, then wrung it out and handed it to me. Dad motioned me to the table. "Keep me posted," he said to the phone, and punched the hang-up button. "You okay, Jeff?"

"Yeah, Dad."

"Then sit down, you two. I have to tell you something."

I sat. "This about Kirby?"

"Yes." He sat too, and pried the cloth from my nose to examine me. He pressed it gently back in place.

"Jeff, an officer tried to get Kirby to pull over, but he wouldn't. He lost him back in the orchards, and now there'll be a warrant on him for failure to stop. But the worst problem he's facing is that now he's also wanted for questioning in Mike's murder."

"I know."

"You know what?"

"That some people think Kirby killed Mike." Berry's head went down. I heard her sniffle.

Mom gasped. "What? You didn't say that," she said to Dad. "Jeff?"

Dad leaned forward on his elbows. "You think it's true?"

"I don't know. He's wearing a scapular. But he says Mike gave it to him. I want to believe him."

"You know about the missing scapular? And now Kirby is wearing one? Jeff, why didn't you tell me?"

I was so tired that the words were an effort, but I wanted it over. "I only found it on him tonight, and I even accused him of killing Mike, but I don't know . . ."

"My God," he said, his voice much softer.

"I think he was running even before the cop went after him. He looked terrified when he left McDonald's." I leaned across the table to Dad. "He's been acting strange. I thought he wanted to talk to me about something. Did I do this to him? Did my accusations push him over?"

"He couldn't have gotten far," Dad said, just like in the movies.

Mom slid quietly up behind me and placed trembling hands on my shoulders. I laid my head back to look up at her. Whatever she saw in my eyes, it made her bend to kiss my forehead.

It wasn't long before Berry and I were sitting with both our fathers in the den, firing off defensive answers to questions. I don't know how she felt at that moment—she never said—but I told Berry later that it couldn't be worse than what a fly feels with a swatter coming at him time and again.

Disappointment reigned supreme, and it was hard, very hard, to find my father beneath the cop.

"If you had come to us sooner—" Cop-Dad said, then stopped, realizing he'd already said the same line several times. "You two, of all people. Anything, anything at all, no matter how insignificant, you know that."

I kept waiting for Berry to gracefully slide the blame to me, but she didn't. So I did it myself.

"Dad, I'm the one who kept putting it off. I couldn't believe it. Kirby killing Mike? How could I accuse him and go to the cops when all I had to go on was dreams? Everything Berry and I came up with came from the dreams. It didn't make sense and it still doesn't, but when I felt the scapular under his shirt, I believed it."

"And now?"

"I don't know how to describe it. I want to believe Mike did give it to him. He looked so awful."

"What about you, Berry?"

Berry's eyes snapped to her father, then back to me. "I know Jeff wants to believe him, but . . . He acts guilty of something for sure. Why did he always ask us what we were doing? Why was he following Jeff?"

It was like a game of Good Kirby, Bad Kirby, with Berry filling in the things I neglected to mention.

"If they don't get him tonight, the chances go down considerably," Mr. Murphy said to no one in particular. We were all aware of the facts that the phone had not rung and the scanner Dad had brought from the bedroom had not given any hope that Kirby's truck had been sighted again.

Mom brought a pot of coffee. She hadn't said a word through any of this but her eyes, the way they went to my father's face when he said anything in a harsh tone, showed plainly that she didn't like it at all. She wouldn't sit down but hung nervously in the doorway, floating first to the kitchen, then to the den.

Dad was stirring creamer into his cup when Berry asked a question of her own. "So, you mean to tell me you never looked at Kirby to begin with?"

Dad's spoon circled slower as he looked at Mr. Murphy to answer.

"Honey, we looked at everybody."

"Kirby didn't seem any more suspicious than anyone else? That's hard to believe, Dad," she said. "You always talk about body language and guilt."

Berry's own body language was like a neon sign. She sat back, one leg tucked under, a pillow on her lap and her arms crossed atop it, shielding herself.

"I mean, gosh," she said, and poked at the corkscrews of dark hair hanging beside her cheek. "Every time we brought Mike up, Kirby would get all fidgety. He answered questions with questions and acted like he was beset with fleas."

That struck me funny and I ducked my head to hide a smile. Only Berry would find someone *beset* with something.

"I could say the same about Jeff," Dad said. "But we knew his reaction was emotional."

I didn't ask whether a killer couldn't have emotions too. I knew it would just start a new tirade in my head about Kirby's weird behavior.

"Well, I don't think there's any more to say," Dad said.

Berry and I exchanged glances and got up. Her dad didn't look like he was ready to go anywhere just yet, and there was something nagging me. I motioned to Berry. We put our coats on and went out back to where the patio furniture was sitting uncovered, under the fine layer of snow.

"I'm glad that's over with," she said, and stepped past me to the edge of the patio. A neighbor's tree, trimmed with white and blue lights, twinkled with a slow rhythm, like a sleeper's heartbeat. The night was still.

"I should apologize now. I'm not good at apologizing unless it's sarcastic, you know. But I feel like all this is my fault. If I hadn't confronted Kirby we'd be plugging along as usual, and we wouldn't be in trouble with our dads."

Berry shrugged, keeping her back to me. "*I* called the cops and started all this. And I'm sorry that we disagree about Kirby to begin with. I can tell how much you care for him."

I stepped up behind her and circled her shoulders with my arms. I laid my head against hers. "I'll probably feel worse before it's over."

She pulled her head back to look at me, then turned in my arms. As her arms went around me I tightened mine.

"Some Christmas this will be," she said into my coat.

"We'll get over it." I thought of the Thayer family, who would be facing their first Christmas without Mike.

She drew away from me and pushed her hair behind her ears. "I've never had Dad this disappointed in me before. But I wouldn't have done it differently. And besides, you would have told eventually."

"Maybe."

"What if it turns out that you're wrong about him?"

I sighed. "I'll face it."

I could tell from her look that she knew what I was leaving unsaid. Something inside me couldn't grasp it, no matter what I'd said to Kirby. And as I stared at the neighbor's tree I was overcome with the feeling that Mike couldn't believe it either.

Chapter 17

The car was quiet as we drove toward the Thayers' house. We had been invited over as a family, to do our annual Thayer–Owens cookie exchange.

"We could have skipped this year," Mom said. She was worried that the Thayers weren't really up to the holiday feel of our visit.

"On the contrary," Dad said. "Ellen made it perfectly clear that they wanted to do it. It will be okay."

Dad's eyes met mine in the rearview mirror.

I felt he was interested in the Kirby-as-killer theory, and I wondered if the police had gotten hints or rumors even before Berry spilled all. But that I'd never learn, because it was pig-story stuff.

At night, when I closed my eyes, I could see Kirby. He was driving. Just driving and shaking his head. He wouldn't look at me. He'd think I did this to him.

Theresa was helping her mother with dinner dishes

when we arrived. The other kids, some in pajamas already, ushered us in and took our coats. Mom carried her containers of cookies into the kitchen and Dad and I joined Mr. Thayer at the fireplace, where he was threading a string of white lights through tufts of evergreen.

"How are you?" Dad asked.

"I'm okay."

Someone tugged on my sleeve and I looked down at Marie. "We're getting a tree next weekend. Do you want to help?"

"I might."

"Are we putting our stockings up, Daddy?"

"Not yet, Marie. Now, stay out of that box."

"I see the manger, Daddy. Are we going to fix the manger?"

Mr. Thayer sighed and handed the string of lights off to Dad. He lifted Marie bodily from the box, which sat inside the empty fireplace. "Look, there's Katy all alone. Go talk to her for a while."

Katy had taken a seat on one end of the sofa and was staring at her hands. She'd gotten upset at the idea of coming to the house and not seeing Mike, and we were all hoping she wouldn't break into tears. Mom was hoping she would see things going on as usual at Mike's house and feel better.

Mom and Mrs. Thayer came into the living room, shooing the boys in front of them. "You'll get your cookies," Mom said. "But let us get them ready first."

I closed my eyes. There was the family noise I remembered from other years. It could be just any year as long as I kept my eyes closed.

I opened them when the cookies and drinks came in on big trays.

"Shall I plug in the lights?" Mr. Thayer asked.

"Yes!" Everyone shouted.

Mom turned out the lamp at her end of the sofa and Mrs. Thayer switched off the one beside her. Soft white light filtered through the evergreen, making all the kids gasp and clap.

Dozens of cookies had been brought out. Mrs. Thayer began baking cookies right after Thanksgiving, freezing them or packing them in tins. Mike used to say he could eat Christmas cookies until Easter.

It was nice. I sat back and enjoyed eating the cookies and hearing the kids' wish lists. Marie slowly made her way to a box near the fireplace.

She pulled a bulky stocking from it and slid its contents into her lap. "I want to set up the manger," she said.

"That goes under the tree, dear." Mrs. Thayer took the figure of Mary from Marie's hands and examined it. "No new chips, thank goodness."

"It can go here," Marie said, patting the hearth.

"Michael? Would it be okay?"

Mr. Thayer nodded. "Let her have her way. We can always move it so Santa won't land on it."

Except for Frank, all the Thayer kids moved to the fireplace to help set up the manger scene. When the figures were in place, the ceramic baby was handed to Mrs. Thayer.

"We need straw," Theresa said. "We didn't get any yet."

"Get some from the broom for now," Mrs. Thayer said.

Theresa ran to the kitchen and came back a minute later with several broom straws sticking out of her fist. "I picked clean ones, Mom," she said.

"So, who puts down the first manger straw?"

"Me!" Marie jumped up and down in front of Theresa.

Theresa looked around. "No, Marie, you helped set up the manger. Frank didn't get to help. Here, Frank." She held the straw toward Frank, who hadn't moved from his chair. He looked sheepishly around the room, then stood.

I didn't know what anyone was expecting, but his parents seemed disappointed in the way he took the straw and plopped it down on the baby's bed. He slunk back to the chair and bit into another cookie.

"I get to do it tomorrow night," Marie said, and sat beside the Holy Family.

"Marie, put this back into a stocking, will you?" Mrs. Thayer held the small infant to her. "He doesn't come until the manger is nice and warm with straw on Christmas Eve."

That got me, for some reason. How many times had I seen the trio of father, mother, and baby set up on lawns, tables, windowsills, and porches? I'd seen them made of plastic, wood, metal, and lights. The Thayers' old ceramic set filled me with a warm feeling.

I went to the kitchen to get eggnog. Theresa followed me with a tray of empty cups. I could tell she wanted to say something.

"How's school?" I asked her as I shook the carton.

"It's okay. Can I ask you something? Mom didn't tell me where Mike was found."

I hadn't expected that. "It doesn't matter, does it?"

"But I know now," she whispered. "A boy in my class said that the haunted barn would have another ghost because Mike was there."

I started to pour. "You don't believe that," I whispered back.

"But that's just it. It could be true."

"No, Theresa."

"I thought it was him, that night at the barn."

I'd never been so shocked by such a little voice. "*Why?*"

"I don't know. It was dark. I did see someone, I really did, and even if it wasn't Mike, that was when I thought he was dead."

She looked ready to cry. I put the carton down and hugged her to me. "I'll tell you a secret, okay? I know that wasn't Mike you saw, because Mike is okay, he's in heaven. He told me he's all right. Don't let anyone tell you that he's a ghost, okay?"

She pulled away and fixed her so-like-Mike eyes on me. "How did he tell you that?"

"In a dream. I've dreamed about him."

"I wish I could see him in a dream."

"You will, I know you will."

She smiled then. We finished pouring and I carried the tray into the living room. Theresa was wearing a big grin. I felt bad for lying to her about the dreams. But I knew that Mike would have done the same.

I watched Marie begin to fall asleep near the fireplace and her manger scene. I watched Frank, who had come out of his funk, join Philip and Jimmy with a Christmas catalog. I watched Theresa braid Katy's hair, the smile still on her face.

Mike was here. He was here in the curl that covered Marie's cheek, in the set of Frank's jaw, and in the soft eyes of his sister Theresa.

And it's hard to describe, but maybe it was because of how easily I could find him here that I felt his absence even more. I glanced at his mother. She was studying Marie, who yawned and leaned dreamily against the wall, and I wondered if her daughter's curly hair held a special attraction for her now.

When we left the house that night, I went away missing Mike more deeply than I had since he'd gone.

— — —

Less than two weeks until Christmas. Mom didn't like to be accused of going overboard, but artificial holly and tiny red bead garlands, draped around evergreen cuttings, and candles appeared on every available flat space.

Katy came home from school excited every day. Her class was counting down to vacation by the minute.

I grew calmer. I could think about Kirby and Mike and not feel the muscles tighten in my jaw or stomach. I hadn't had a headache in several days. I was enjoying every moment of feeling fine. I told Berry about it.

We were sitting in the mall, keeping an eye on Deena and Katy. They were in line to see Santa. Berry listened to me and said, "It's because we told, came clean."

"Think so?"

"Sure. I've been feeling good too. No looking for hidden agendas when Dad asks me what I've been up to, and I'm not hunting up work schedules or trying to remember who I can say what to."

Maybe that was it. I put an arm around her and we waited for the girls to have their turns on Santa's lap.

Then we took the girls to the Christmas movie. Berry and I watched some of it, but most of the time was spent with our heads together, watching the way light danced over each other's eyes and writing letters in each other's palms. It was silly, and it felt so very nice.

If people still watched me in school, I stopped noticing. I was concentrating better, getting things done. Out of all the class changes in a day, there would be only one or two where I caught myself looking at the walls of lockers, thinking of number 1121.

I heard a few guys ask about Kirby during lunch. His father had called a couple of them to ask if he'd been around. I wondered why Mr. Kirby hadn't called me. Or if he had, why I hadn't been told.

For two nights I worked on college applications. Things were normal, almost too normal.

At lunch on Friday I asked Berry if she wanted to hang out with me that night.

"Sure," she said. "Where?"

"I don't know."

"Want to come to my house and play pool?"

"No."

"Should I come to your house?"

"No."

"Well, I don't have any money, Jeff, except to buy Christmas presents."

"Same here." We laughed and she shook her head.

"Then what can we do?"

"Let's just go for a ride. Look at the lights and talk."

"Sure. What time?"

"After supper. Since we're both broke, we should eat first." She laughed again.

I was a little worried. Without Mike and Kirby, without watching our sisters at a silly movie, with no other distraction, could Berry and I be just Berry and I?

I only knew that something had changed between us when I kissed her in the car, as she cried the night of the winter cookout.

That night, when I picked her up, I had scrounged up some money.

Deena opened the door and ran to get Berry. Mr. Murphy was sitting on the sofa. I hadn't seen him since he and Dad had questioned us and shaken their heads in that devastated way. He smiled at me. "Sit down while you wait."

"That's okay." For the first time in my life I felt uncomfortable in the Murphys' home.

Then Berry appeared. "Hi, Jeff."

She looked pretty, in a fuzzy white sweater and with her hair pulled back by a wide white band. As she passed me to get her coat, I caught a hint of vanilla. She put on perfume for me? To ride around in the car?

"Let's drive through the developments to see the lights, okay?" she asked.

"Deal. Then we'll get some dessert."

We drove around and made comments on the decorations. I kept waiting for this really terrific conversation to begin, but it didn't.

It wasn't until we were at the diner that we actually had to talk. Berry started.

"I'm going for my driver's license during vacation. Mom's taking me."

"That's great. You'll pass with no trouble at all."

"Well, I know that," she said.

I searched for something else to say. "We're going to get a tree tomorrow."

"What time are you going?"

"I'm not sure. We're going to meet the Thayers."

"Oh yeah! Did you see Mr. Kirby on the news this evening?"

"Kirby's father? No."

"It wasn't much. A reporter went to the garage to talk to him. Asked him if he thought Kirby's running was connected to Mike. It was sick, really. I mean, why bother him?"

Dad had said it wouldn't be long before a reporter got wind of it. I was surprised it had taken a week. "What did Mr. Kirby say?"

"He just said that none of it was proven. He finally got away from the guy."

"Reporters. Like them or not, they sure find things out. But let's not talk about Kirby or Mike. Let's talk about something else."

"Like what? Oh, here's our cake."

We ate quietly for a minute.

"Tell me what's on your mind, Jeff."

Yeah, I thought, tell her. So I took a deep breath. "It's dumb, I know, but I was afraid that if we didn't have the Mike thing to talk about, well, maybe we wouldn't be able to talk at all." I studied my plate. "When you brought up the news, I thought I'd never find out."

Berry laughed softly, slid her hand over to cover mine. "I'm happy just spending time with you. I'm sure we could talk for hours, if that's what you want. As far as that topic goes, well, it's going to come up sometimes, especially now since the news broke."

"You're right."

I didn't even want to think about what school would be like on Monday. Everybody would know that Kirby was wanted for questioning, and they would be watching to see how I was taking it.

Would it ever, *ever* be over?

Chapter 18

Saturday was a great day, cold and clear. The small pine-covered hills outside town made the Christmas-tree farm look like an orderly forest. We waited in the parking lot for the Thayers, Katy hopping up and down with eagerness. "Here they are!" she shouted as their van pulled in.

We all hugged as our dads went to get the tree saws from the man who ran the farm. Then we took off behind them, heading for the hill of Scotch pines.

Frank hung back, eyes on the ground as he walked. He was wearing the same sullen look he had had the night we exchanged cookies.

I felt torn. Maybe Frank needed to talk to someone; maybe I could help. On the other hand, no one else seemed concerned about his mood, so why should I bother?

Because.

I slipped between two trees and waited for everyone else to pass me, then stepped onto the path beside Frank. He didn't seem to notice, or care.

"Hey, Frank, how's it going?"

"Okay."

"What have you been up to?"

"Nothing. School."

I was just thinking that the best thing might be to leave him alone when he looked up.

"Hey, Jeff?"

"Yeah?"

"Do you want the Chevy?"

"What? Heck no, that's your car now."

"Well, I don't want it anymore, so do you?"

"No, I . . . Why don't you want it? You were excited about it before. What happened?"

Frank stopped in his tracks. "Jerry happened."

Oh, God. The news had gotten to the kids. Frank was angry now, and would be for the rest of his life, perhaps. But one day he would think of the car as a connection to Mike, the way he had before, and he'd be sorry it was gone.

"Look, I'll make a deal with you, Frank."

"What is it?"

"You know I'd love to work on the car, but I don't have a place to keep it. We don't have an extra garage or shed, and I can't leave it to sit outside. That would just undo all the work Mike put into it. So, what if I said I'd work on it if you'd let me keep it there?"

He considered it for a while. "I guess that's okay."

"You sure?"

"Yeah, I'm sure."

"Could you help me sometimes? 'Cause I imagine it gets kind of boring out there by yourself."

Frank shook his head. "Mike, he never got bored."

"Well, Mike was different than most people, wasn't he?"

Frank nodded, bit his lip.

I searched for a word. "Mike was . . ."

Frank stood straight, pushed his chin up at me. "Mike was the best." His pride said it all.

"That's right. Come on."

We ran to catch up with the others. I had put a bandage on his hurt. That was all I could do for now.

Mom was putting dishes in the dishwasher while I scooped the last of the egg custard out of its bowl.

"Are you finished with that?" Mom asked.

"Just." I handed her the bowl.

"Are you going out tonight with Berry?"

"We didn't plan to."

"Didn't you have fun last night?"

"Yes, but—"

"Why don't you invite her for dinner tomorrow? She can help us put up the tree."

"Okay. I'll call her later."

After my confession at the diner last night, Berry and

I had gotten along fine. We'd talked about all kinds of things.

That was one of the things I missed with Mike gone. We used to talk for hours, sometimes about nothing, but we could talk, going from subject to subject. Everybody needs someone like that. Everybody has to have someone to run off at the mouth with.

What would happen to someone who didn't have anybody to talk to? Did they all end up like the old lady who lived in the one-room efficiency over the drugstore? How many times had I seen her hanging out the window in all kinds of weather, yelling to people on the street? When she died, her body lay for two days before anyone found her. Dad said people were so used to tuning her out that she had become invisible.

Mom said being invisible was like being dead.

I shook myself, not wanting to slip back into the depression I had felt myself coming out of. And I realized, now, that it had been a depression brought on by grief and tension and who knew what else. As the depression began to lift, its side effects, headaches and lethargy, had eased. I didn't want them back.

I went to my room and put a CD on. Lying on the bed, I looked around. The calendar caught my eye. I had hung it back up and turned it to the correct month. I thought about all the days that had slipped past me. They were bunched into one block, one jumbled clump of fear and hurt and bad times.

Things had to go one day at a time now. I couldn't let the little jolts of bad clump together to take away my days anymore.

Like on Friday, when school was over. I was thinking about Berry, worried about how things would go that night, if we could talk. Regular, normal worries compared to everything else. Then, as I was leaving, I passed the office door just as a secretary was taking down the sign about crisis counselors.

It stopped me cold. *Mike's dead!* something screamed in me, and my jaw clenched tight. I made my way outside with everyone else, thinking, *I know that. I will always know it, no matter what I do or where I go.* Heading home, I realized that the hardest part of all would be to accept it, make that frozen moment by the office be just that: one bad moment.

Now I thought of Kirby. He was caught in a jumble of bad, like I had been. I got sleepy, turned my face into my pillow.

I must have been falling asleep when I heard Mike, far away.

"Watch out for Kirby," he said. Over and over.

All evening I thought about Berry. I wanted to tell her about how I had heard Mike's voice, but I didn't know whether I should or not. When I woke up from the nap I could remember the voice, but there wasn't a dream to go with it. I felt lonely, so I called Berry around eight.

"Mom says to ask you to dinner tomorrow. Eat with us and help decorate our tree. What do you say?"

"Do you always do what your mom says?"

"When I like the idea, yeah."

"Will you pick me up?"

"Of course."

All these little silences crept into our conversation and I thought of all the things I should be saying to her. Like, I wished I could see her face-to-face, because hearing her voice and laughing with her still left me lonely somehow.

When we hung up I couldn't shake the feeling. I asked Dad for the car and told him I was going to drive over there to see her. And I really thought I was. But once I was on the road, I found myself driving in a different direction. When I saw the arched entryway of the cemetery coming up on my right, I knew where I'd been wanting to go all along.

I parked on the curve closest to Mike's grave. I hadn't been up to the cemetery since the funeral, and although that day was clear in my mind, I wasn't sure I could find the right spot in the dark. The flashlight we kept in the car needed new batteries. It cast a weak beam over the ground.

The night was quiet there on the hill; there was no

sound other than the traffic out on the main road behind me. I headed in what I thought was the right direction and played the flashlight back and forth until I found it. There was no stone yet, only the small metal marker staked in by the cemetery. The Thayers had said they would put a stone up in the spring, when the ground was warm.

Two poinsettias leaned toward each other. A glimmer of gold shone from a card that said *Brother* in fancy script.

I stood there, wanting to say so much, but my breath streamed away in a silent mist. Maybe it would be enough for me now to just stand in his company.

I could feel him, just like I had at the Thayers' house. If I closed my eyes I could feel him near me. Questions went through my head. Was he really aware of us? Berry seemed to think he was, she had said so on the bleachers that day. So, did he see me standing here now? Did he know where Kirby was?

I shifted on my cold feet, turned the flashlight off, and pulled my hands up into my sleeves. "Why can't you tell me?" I asked out loud. "If you could tell me all that other stuff in the dreams, why can't you come out and give me a name? Tell me what happened?"

I shivered and bit down on my lips to keep my teeth from chattering. "Damn it, Mike, help me out, will you? Are you here?"

I closed my eyes and waited. My heart fluttered,

missed a beat. I could feel him. I was straining so hard to hear a voice that the air seemed to buzz around me. The back of my neck tingled and I thought I heard a movement behind me.

I didn't turn. I froze.

"Mike?"

Something landed on the ground near my feet. My heart stopped. Then I switched on the flashlight and stared at the brown scapular.

A hand came down on my shoulder. "It ain't Mike," Kirby said.

Chapter 19

I jumped sideways and swung the light into Kirby's face.

"Sorry," he said.

I took a deep breath, tried to stop the shaking in my arms and legs. "What . . . ?"

"Can we talk?"

"Did you follow me here?"

"It doesn't matter, does it?"

I pointed at the scapular. "What's with that?"

"It's his."

Suddenly I was sweating in my coat. *He lied! He lied to me!* "You said he gave it to you."

"This one," he said, slapping his chest like Mike had done in the dream. "He gave me this one a long time ago. But that one is his."

I couldn't catch my breath. I was panting like I'd run a

race. "But, then, that means . . ." I started to back away and he grabbed my arm.

"Don't think, Jeff. Just listen, okay? Just listen to me. It's not true. I mean, it is, but . . . Christ, Jeff, I didn't mean it, I swear, and I can tell you what really happened that night, but you gotta promise to hear me out and let me take care of things, take care of it. Will you do that? Will you listen?"

I was frozen again. Voices screamed in my head: *Run! No, listen to him; you wanted to know what happened. Watch Kirby; watch yourself.*

"This is killing me, Jeff."

His head drooped. He let go of me.

Kirby looked bad. His dirty hair hung in heavy strands and he hadn't shaved in days. He seemed close to tears. When I saw the way his hands were shaking, I felt the muscles in my shoulders relax and I believed him.

"Let's go to the car," I said. We walked over, me one step behind.

He shivered as he shut the door and settled back into the seat. I cracked the window open a bit to dispel his smell of wet wool, smoke, and beer.

"You look terrible, Kirby. I've never seen you like this."

"Yeah, well, I don't feel too great right now. I can't believe you set the cops on me, man. I thought we were friends, you know?"

He didn't sound mean, it was more like a whine. I stopped being afraid. "Berry called them."

"I'm sorry if I hurt you that night."

"Same here."

"Can I smoke?"

I was caught off guard by Kirby's asking permission to do anything. "Open the window."

Sighing, he rolled the window down. He squinted at me over the lighter's flame. "You've got to believe me."

"I will."

I gripped the steering wheel and leaned my head against the window, looked out into the darkness so I wouldn't have to look at him. I was afraid of what I'd hear, but more afraid of never knowing.

"Ever since it happened, I've been blaming Rick."

"Rick Whitman has something to do with Mike?"

"Listen to me, then you decide for yourself, okay? See, I'd been letting Rick park cars at the junkyard overnight. He'd bring a different license plate and get the car the next day, and pay me twenty bucks for the favor."

I kept my eyes away from him. Something told me to stay quiet while he talked, no matter what he said.

"Mike was coming to the yard then, had been for months, getting parts for his Chevy and just tinkering around. He finally told me he knew what Rick was doing, that the cars were stolen. He asked me what Dad would do if he found out. Dad doesn't go in the yard anymore.

"Anyway, I told him to mind his business. But you know Mike." He sighed.

"He told me I ought to watch who I let do what, that Dad could lose the place if Rick got hauled in one day and brought me into it. And it got me to thinking. Not that I told him that, you know. Instead, I told him I'd take care of it."

Kirby coughed, then rolled the window up. "Like I said, Mike kept coming by, and he didn't press it, but he let me know it when he noticed one of Rick's cars. It kind of made me feel guilty, but I knew he wouldn't tell anybody. Then, one night . . ."

Kirby sniffed, coughed again. He shifted in the seat. I closed my eyes.

He cleared his throat. "This one night Rick came in the yard. I saw him and followed him back. He was throwing the tarp off this red Ford and opening the trunk. I walked up to him.

"There were boxes in the trunk, Jeff, and he opened one and I saw all these cellophane bags."

I felt him turn in the seat to look at me, but I didn't move.

"Well, I slammed the trunk closed. 'What the hell are you doing?' I yelled. 'Hey man,' he said. 'I'm gonna give you a bonus!' All the stuff Mike had been telling me came over me in a rush. It's one thing to tarp a car in the yard, you know? But if he's stealing cars from drug dealers and putting them in my yard, I got a lot more than cops to worry about!

"I told him to get the hell out and not bother coming back. He just laughed, told me he'd give me more money. I pushed him, told him to get out, and he just kept his ground, said he'd go when it got good and dark.

"It was getting dark, but I didn't want him hanging around while I had to watch the station, maybe hiding some of his stuff around the yard. I got so angry I went into the station, and when I came back I had my dad's gun."

It was coming. The thing that had been haunting me, haunting us all for months, was coming, and I was going to hear it first.

"Rick looked at me and the gun but didn't move. I pointed it at him, told him I'd shoot holes through the car if he didn't get in it and go now. He moved to the door. But then Mike stepped out from behind a pile of old tires. He said, 'Kirby, drop the gun!'

"I hadn't seen him come into the yard! Rick started yelling, wanting to know who the hell it was. Mike told him to go or he'd call the cops. Rick started toward him and pulled Mike over by the car, tugging on his shirt and yelling at him. I told him to leave Mike alone, but I didn't go closer because of the gun. Rick was shaking him; Mike was trying to stay on his feet. Rick laughed at him, said he wasn't gonna tell anybody, was he?

"I'd never shot that gun before, Jeff. . . . I wasn't gonna shoot it!" He took a deep breath. "Mike said to put it down. Then Rick tried to grab it. I don't know why he tried to grab it, I wasn't gonna shoot it, I just wanted him out of there!"

Kirby was crying now, and I could feel the tightness in my throat.

"Rick grabbed it . . . it went off in my hand. I swear, Jeff, I didn't know Mike had been hit. I thought he was by the car, but he must have started heading for the gates. I didn't know he was hit until Rick let go and jumped in the car. I watched him pull forward, then to the gates.

"It was dark then. I saw this body lying there. . . . It was Mike. He was dead."

I saw the scuffle, saw the gun go off and Mike going down. Tears were running down my face, but I didn't move.

"I should have called the police, but I was afraid. I shot the gun. I killed him. I panicked. All I could think of was to close the garage and get Mike out of there. It was awful. I'd never been so afraid before. Mike was dead and I'd done it.

"I thought I'd move him, put him somewhere so I could think, figure out what to do. Then I thought of the woods behind the barn. I put him in my truck. Oh, God, *Mike* . . ."

Kirby put his hand on my arm. "Jeff, I was almost

wishing a cop would stop me so it would be over. But it didn't happen, and the longer I went without saying something, the more impossible it was to do." He stopped. "I found that thing—what's it called? A scapular? It was in the yard, it must have come off when Rick was shaking him. It's like the one he gave me.

"And so much happened . . . I need to get it over with."

I turned to him then. "It's not over, Kirby. It won't ever be over."

Kirby's face was wet and he nodded. "I know. He comes to me, you know? He does."

Oh my God, I thought. "In dreams?"

Kirby shook his head. "I . . . I see him. I know you won't believe me, but I see him. I went back once, to the barn. Just to check, because I thought, hey, maybe this is some weird game he's playing on me now. Maybe he's alive, trying to teach me a lesson, you know? But he was there. It was awful. I'm telling the truth, and maybe you'll believe me if I tell you I saw your car there."

I swallowed. "On Halloween?"

"Yeah. I was going to call to you, but then I saw the kids. You didn't see me?"

"No, Kirby, I didn't."

Mike had said that Kirby didn't help. Not that Kirby didn't come to him.

"I think I'm going crazy," Kirby said, and started sobbing. He held his head and rocked in the seat. "I didn't mean it."

"I believe you."

"Good. Good, I'm glad." He dragged a sleeve over his eyes. "Maybe Mike will leave me alone now, maybe he'll stop."

Then something clicked in me, and I knew what Mike had meant about watching Kirby. And I knew why Kirby was seeing him.

"Kirby, what did you do with the gun?"

"I've got it hidden."

"Doesn't your dad wonder where it is?"

Kirby sniffed, lit another cigarette. "He never opens the box," he said, letting out a stream of smoke.

"Why did you keep it?"

"At first I was gonna use it on Rick. But I never found the bastard. And now . . ."

"Now?"

Kirby looked me in the eye, then raised a forefinger to his head.

"Mike doesn't want that. He wasn't trying to drive you crazy, either. He was watching out for you."

He laughed. "Yeah, right. Who's crazy here?"

"Mike loved you, Kirby. I think he still does. He doesn't want you to do anything stupid, he even told me to watch you, in one of those dreams I had."

"But I killed him."

"It was an accident. And he forgave you the very second the gun went off."

"How do you know that?"

"He told me."

Kirby closed his eyes. I could feel that he believed me. It didn't matter that Mike hadn't told me that in so many words. He'd told me that in the way his death made me visit his church and learn how much he loved it. He'd told me that in the way he trusted me with his messages.

"What do I do now?" Kirby asked.

"I think you know."

He sighed. "Why'd he do it, huh, Jeff? Why did he come out from behind those tires to play tough guy, huh?"

"I guess it was something he had to do."

We sat in silence.

Finally Kirby said, "It's starting to snow."

After a while I started the car. As we left the cemetery I couldn't help noticing the way Kirby peered out the window. He seemed to be searching for something, or someone, out in the darkness.

Chapter 20

I talked Kirby into coming home with me to tell Dad his story. My house would be a lot less threatening than the police station. If Dad knew Kirby's situation, he'd treat him fairly.

The house was dark except for the light over the kitchen sink. Kirby walked in behind me willingly.

"Dad can't be asleep yet. You head into the shower, I'll make coffee. Dad will lend you some clothes."

As I walked into my parents' room I tried not to guess how Dad would react. I jumped when he spoke out of the dark.

"Who do you have out there, Jeff?"

I whispered, in case Mom was asleep. "Jerry Kirby. We want to talk to you."

Whatever it was he said, it came out like he was being strangled. As he grabbed up a pair of sweatpants from the floor I asked him for a clean pair for Kirby. I opened the bathroom door to throw them onto the sink.

It wasn't easy to convince Dad not to call the station right away. I gave him a brief rundown of Kirby's story. Dad still wasn't sure, but I swayed him with the argument that he should trust my instincts when it came to handling Kirby.

Dad and I were sitting at the kitchen table when Kirby came in. He and Dad stared at each other while I got up to pour coffee all around.

Kirby spoke first. "Did you call anybody?"

"Not yet," Dad said, pointing to a chair. "Drink your coffee first. There's plenty of time."

Whether it was Kirby's wet hair or reddened eyes I didn't know, but Dad ordered me to fetch him a sweatshirt and heavy socks. When I came back, Dad was talking quietly to him.

"So, what do I call you?"

"Kirby's fine."

"How old are you, Kirby?"

"Eighteen. On August twenty-ninth." Kirby slipped the sweatshirt over his head and sipped the coffee.

"Okay," Dad said. "I'm not sure what Jeff told you, if anything, but you should know that whatever you say to me—"

"Mr. Owens, I know all that. I'm gonna be telling it fifty times, so I don't have to say it all now. It's just that Jeff told me you'd take me down to the station yourself."

"Dad, when he said he'd go in, I sort of told him you'd go with him, so they know he's serious, really trying."

Kirby seemed to shrink inside himself, hunching over the table, cradling his coffee close to his chest. His jaw clenched, making little muscles wriggle beneath the skin.

"It's all got to stop now," Kirby said. "I can't go on like this, and if I hadn't caught up with Jeff, I would have killed myself. And never told about Mike. But you've got to find Rick Whitman, because he can tell you that what I'm saying is the truth."

"Do you have any idea where Rick Whitman is?" Dad asked.

"No. I wish I did."

"We'll talk to his family."

Kirby snorted.

"Berry saw his sister talking to him not that long ago," I said.

Kirby looked at me in surprise.

"I was afraid to tell you, and now I'm glad I didn't."

"So what do we do now?" Kirby asked Dad.

"Are you turning yourself in to me?"

"Yes, sir."

"Okay. Have another cup of coffee, then we'll go. I'll call in to say we'll be there shortly."

Dad got up, patted Kirby on the shoulder, then went to the phone.

"Can I smoke?"

I glanced at Dad, caught his nod.

"Yeah, sure, Kirby."

I dozed off and on, wrapped in a blanket on the recliner. The only light came from the television turned to a music video station, its volume low. Dad came home around two A.M.

"I thought you'd be in bed," he said, and threw his coat over the arm of the sofa.

"Couldn't sleep. What about Kirby?"

He sat on the edge of the sofa. "He gave his confession, and it was consistent with what you told me."

"I think he would have killed himself, like he said."

Dad sighed, then yawned. "Hard to tell. But you wouldn't want to take the chance. When his father came in, Kirby bawled like a baby."

"I've been thinking. I tried to put myself in his shoes, live the story through his eyes. You know, he always treated me and Mike like we were little kids—like little brothers. Killing Mike by accident . . . He was terrified."

Dad nodded. "It's tearing him up. He told us he threw the gun away at first because it killed Mike. But when he ran away he went searching for it. He wanted to die with that same gun. Luckily, he came upon you first."

"Are they going to watch him?"

"For a few days."

"What about Rick?"

"We won't forget Mr. Whitman. He'll be answering some questions when we get him."

"Do you have any idea what Kirby's facing?"

"His negligence lies in the fact that he brought a weapon onto the scene. But he did not intentionally pull the trigger. Right now, as long as we can get Whitman to corroborate Kirby's story, which I imagine he will eventually, Kirby could be tried for manslaughter. Accidental death. He will probably serve some jail time, but then, I'm not a lawyer."

"You believe him too." I felt relief settle on me.

"I want to. I trust your instincts."

"Thanks, for everything. For believing us, and for taking him down and staying with him."

"I did what I could."

"You know, Berry kept telling me we should have been open with you from the beginning, and if we had been, maybe Kirby would have confessed."

"Maybe. But it's done now, so rest easy. And speaking of rest, I think we should both go to bed."

"You go ahead. If I wake up in time I'm going to go to early mass. Okay?"

"Early mass," he said, yawning. "Sounds okay, son." He slipped quietly down the hall.

"You did good, Mike," I whispered.

I did go to mass, and driving home in the bright sunshine, I felt the lack of sleep. I got home and went to bed, and slept so hard and long that at dinnertime Dad went to get Berry. Mom woke me when she arrived. We ate and did the tree thing and had a good time. I knew that when we had a moment alone Berry would pester me about my meeting with Kirby. I'd kiss her then.

That night I was able to fall asleep easily. Waking up to Monday and school was a bit harder. I didn't look forward to it, especially after seeing my name on the front page of the paper! I hadn't given any information to anyone except Dad, yet there I was, being partly credited with Kirby's turning himself in to the cops.

By lunchtime, though, I had to admit that it wasn't as bad as I had feared. Instead of the angry remarks I had expected about Kirby and what he'd done to Mike, or the threats I thought I'd have to shoulder from Kirby's friends, people were pretty much leaving me alone.

I talked to Berry about it. "All I have to do is say, 'It was an accident,' and they nod. Why do those words seem to be the magic formula?"

"Because they come from you, Jeff."

"So?" I really didn't get it.

"Jeff," she said, laying a warm palm on my hand and shaking her head. "It's because of who you are. You're Mike's best friend. They figure that if you truly believe it was an accident they should too. And no one wants to believe Kirby did it on purpose."

"I never believed it."

She smiled. "No, you never did."

"And what about you?"

"This is still terrible. Mike is still gone. But I'm glad you're such a good judge of character."

"Yeah," I said, and kissed her.

I kept expecting another dream, a final farewell, if you will. But each night I slept straight through and woke up disappointed. Three days before Christmas, Theresa called to ask me to the children's service on Christmas Eve. She was going to sing in the choir.

Afterward I followed them home. Mr. Thayer put a Christmas tape on the stereo and helped his wife convince the kids to go up and change into pajamas.

When they'd gone upstairs, he had me follow him to the kitchen, where he started to make some cocoa.

"Jeff, I don't know how to express myself here, but there's something I have to say to you."

His calm voice told me not to worry. "Go ahead."

"I'm still not sure of my feelings about what has happened. Jerry Kirby sat at my table. He got Frank all excited about working on the car. And he did it all with my son's blood on his hands. I want to hate him for that, but how can I show hate in front of my children? If our faith means anything, I'm supposed to forgive him."

"I know."

"They said he was suicidal. Was he?"

"I think so."

"That makes it easier to forgive. Is that a terrible thing to say?"

"No, Mr. Thayer."

He pulled mugs from the dish drainer and smiled. "And you? Do you forgive him?"

This man deserved the best answer I could give. "I've learned something lately. There are things I don't understand, and will never understand, but that doesn't mean they aren't possible. And accepting those things instead of questioning them brings me peace.

"In the same way . . . I know that Mike is dead, and that Kirby caused it. I have to accept it. I'm hoping that if I can do that, the acceptance will bring me peace, and peace will let me forgive."

He smiled. "You talk like Mike."

"Jeff! Come on, Daddy, hurry." It was Marie, in a peppermint-striped flannel gown. "We want to bring the baby out."

We followed her to the living room.

"We need tonight's straw," Theresa said. "Let's make it perfect."

"Is there anybody who wants to do it?" Mrs. Thayer asked.

"I want to do the baby," Marie said.

"And you will," her mother said. She reached down into the toe of Theresa's stocking and pulled the ceramic infant out.

"That's where you hid him! I thought it was the orange you let me put in each one." Marie held her hands out.

Everybody laughed at her surprise, and Mrs. Thayer said to me, "We had to hide it because she wanted to carry it around constantly."

The crèche was set up under the tree, the manger nearly invisible under bits of straw. Theresa appeared beside me. "Who's going to put the last bit of straw down?"

No one spoke up. I looked at her.

"Let's have Jeff do it," she said.

Everyone was waiting for me to make a move. Mrs. Thayer smiled. "Would you?"

I took the short pieces of straw from Theresa's hand and knelt down in front of the manger scene. It came from left field, the funny chill on my neck when I placed the straw around the crib. I felt Mike's nearness; then for a moment I *was* Mike, not Jeff standing proxy for him in a family tradition. I felt the oneness of the family, knew without looking that the small hand on my shoulder belonged to Philip. Maybe I was taking too long in nudging the straw into place, but then, somehow I knew that this was just the way Mike would do it, wanting his brothers and sisters to see that he did it seriously, with care and with . . . faith.

Then Mike was gone and it was just me arranging straw for the kids. I felt suddenly empty.

"There," I said, standing up. "How's that?"

"Good," Marie said. "Now me with the baby."

"Now you, honey," her father said.

I left after the kids were sent up to get ready for bed. Mr. Thayer walked me out.

"It'll be an hour yet before there's no more noise from upstairs," he said. "Then—Santa! The presents are stashed in our neighbor's garage."

"Thanks for letting me come over tonight, Mr. Thayer."

"You never need an invitation, Jeff. Have a nice Christmas." He hugged me, then let me go.

"You too."

I drove to the cemetery. I wanted to visit Mike's grave with no questions burning in my mind.

It was windy, but the sky was clear. I brushed snow from the new poinsettias. New cards, tied to the flowers with ribbons, said *Brother* and *Son*. They fluttered in the wind.

"Hey, Mike," I said aloud. "It's okay. You don't have to answer me. I know you can hear me and that's all that matters.

"Berry says I don't have to understand a concept to accept it. She's right. And I don't know if I'll ever understand the dreams or the way you took care of Kirby. But you don't have to do that anymore. I'll watch him for you. I'll be there for your family, too. We'll be together on that, like brothers ought to be.

"I used to ask you when all this would be over. I told Kirby it would never be, but maybe I'm wrong, because you're home now. You're not 'nowhere' anymore. In any case, I'll never say good-bye to you."

The wind was cold on my face, but I stood there a little longer. The cards flapped noisily, then one broke loose. It wrapped itself around my ankle, and I reached for it before it could fly away. I shined the light on it.

Brother.

I held it to my face for a long time.

"Merry Christmas to you too, Mike."

I drove home feeling a little spark of joy. It had been months since I'd felt it, but I recognized it right away. If I hurried, I could catch Katy awake and tell her I'd seen weird lights in the sky. And heard something in the wind that sounded like bells.

About the Author

Shelley Sykes lives with her family in Arendtsville, Pennsylvania, in orchard country, where she enjoys investigating haunted houses. She has worked as a newspaper correspondent and columnist.

For Mike was chosen as the Honor Book in the Fourteenth Annual Delacorte Press Prize contest for a first young adult novel.